OUT OF MIND

ALSO BY DAVID BERGEN

Here the Dark

Stranger

Leaving Tomorrow

The Age of Hope

The Matter with Morris

The Retreat

The Time in Between

The Case of Lena S.

See the Child

A Year of Lesser

Sitting Opposite My Brother

OUT OF MIND

—a novel—

DAVID BERGEN

GOOSE LANE

Edited by Bethany Gibson.
Cover and page design by Julie Scriver.
Cover images: morguefile.com
Printed in Canada by Friesens.
10 9 8 7 6 5 4 3 2 1

Library and Archives Canada Cataloguing in Publication

Title: Out of mind : a novel / David Bergen.
Names: Bergen, David, 1957- author.
Identifiers: Canadiana (print) 20210176598 | Canadiana (ebook) 20210176601 |
ISBN 9781773102160 (softcover) | ISBN 9781773102177 (EPUB)
Classification: LCC PS8553.E665 O98 2021 | DDC C813/.54—dc23

Goose Lane Editions acknowledges the generous support of the Government of
Canada, the Canada Council for the Arts, and the Government of New Brunswick.

Goose Lane Editions
500 Beaverbrook Court, Suite 330
Fredericton, New Brunswick
CANADA E3B 5X4
gooselane.com

In August, on her way to France for a wedding, Lucille first went to Thailand to visit her daughter Libby. The trip to Bangkok included a lengthy layover in Hong Kong, and so Lucille took a room in the city. She slept poorly due to the jet lag and the pounding of music that rose through her floor from the bar below. Just as the sun was rising, she walked out of the hotel and explored the nearby streets. In a square, she found a noodle stand and sat on a small metal stool and watched old women doing tai chi. The light was creeping between the buildings, the cars and motorcycles were cacophonous. Beside her stool were cages with live chickens. The soup was strange and delicious, the presence of the chickens was strange, and she herself was a stranger. She liked the anonymity.

On the plane ride from Los Angeles to Hong Kong, she had been upgraded to business class because the seat she had been assigned had been double-booked. And so, she found herself luxuriating near the front of the plane. She settled in. She asked for a glass of red wine. Another. She removed her headphones when the plane prepared for takeoff. The man seated behind her was telling his neighbour that his wife, in their marriage, was forever crossing boundaries. These were boundaries of control and jealousy. It was hard to live with a woman who existed on the edge of madness and was constantly scouring his phone and his email. He said that his wife had all his passwords. Because he gave them to her. She would have torn her hair out had he not. No choice.

She dozed off to the sound of his voice, and when she woke, he was still talking. And then, as if he had been throttled mid-speech, the man stopped. He had fallen asleep. Everyone around her was now sleeping. The clink of silverware and glasses was a comforting sound from the galley behind the curtains. A hostess approached and offered her a warm cloth. She took it and pressed it against her face and brow. She felt guilty for the ecstasy of luxury. She asked the hostess for a second cloth. When it came, she simply held it between her palms. In the last while, she felt she had been clinging to the wall of a cliff, full of dread. Reason did not calm her, thinking about her desires, her fears, her distress, just made her more anxious, and sleep was hard to find.

Certainly, much of the dread had to do with her daughter Libby. Three months earlier, Libby had travelled to Southeast Asia — because it was the least expensive destination — and while there, she had fallen in with a group of young people who were led by a man named Shane. The group lived in Pattaya, on a compound where they shared food and chores and money, and they hired local teachers to give Thai classes, and they taught English in turn, and it all might have been a paradise, except that, in Lucille's mind, one person's paradise was another's hell. Libby had a propensity for leaping before looking, and now it seemed that she was leaping into the arms of Shane. Libby had sent a photo of her and Shane. On the beach.

In street clothes. He wore a long-sleeved blue shirt, flip-flops, and wide blue pants that fell mid-calf. She wore a misshapen dress. Her face looked thinner, her hair was in a single braid. They were leaning into each other, which was meant to be a sure sign of something, but to Lucille it simply indicated codependence. Stand up straight, she muttered at the photo.

And then, just last week, Libby had called Lucille, asking for advice, but not really asking, just wanting to talk. She was in love. With a man who was brilliant and who had even mentioned marriage. But she wasn't sure if it was right. And yet she felt that it was completely right. She was thinking of taking a year off from medical school. It would be allowed. She could gather her thoughts. Make sense of what she wanted.

What is it you want? Lucille asked.

I don't know, Libby wailed. I don't know.

This must be hard, Lucille said.

Would you come here? To visit? Libby asked.

I can't now, Libby. I have work. I have August free, but I plan to go to the south of France.

Why?

A wedding of a friend.

You have friends in France? Libby asked. She might as well have said, You have friends? such was the astonishment.

I do.

Couldn't you miss it?

We'll talk more.

I don't have any money left, Mom.

9

How about him? Could he help out?

His name is Shane. And no, I couldn't ask him. He works so hard, and all of his money goes to the group. Just a small e-transfer. I'll pay you back.

You must think about yourself and what is best for you, Lucille said. Not just today, but three years from now. Ten years from now. Feelings are just that, feelings. Now you have to think.

Okay, Mom, Libby said. I will.

Take your time. You don't need to decide about marriage. Not today or tomorrow, or even this month. Do you have someone there to talk to? Someone outside the group?

No. Just Shane. He's very wise. But he is also impatient. And he loves me.

Run like hell, thought Lucille. She said that she would transfer the money.

And here Lucille now was, on her way to Bangkok and then to Pattaya, where she would face her daughter.

Marriage — the act, the idea, the romance, the obligation, the foolhardiness, the fiction — was coming at her from all sides. She had been married. She was no longer. She had two grown daughters who were not yet settled. She had a grandchild, Jake, a boy of eleven. She was a psychiatrist who offered psychotherapy instead of prescriptions. She dealt in grief, in pain, in the currency of the self, and, especially of late, in the disappointment of marriage. Contrary to what some might think, no relationship was in any way exceptional. You think that your unhappiness is special? Think again. Read Tolstoy, she had told one of her patients, the same woman who kept asking for suggestions for self-help books. Here, she said, reaching behind her and then turning and placing *Family Happiness* in the woman's hands.

It was almost effortless for years to slip by in a marriage, during which *relations to one another remained unchanged and seemed to have taken a fixed shape which could not become either better or worse.* Some took comfort in this. Others ran. Still others adulterated what little fixed shape remained.

This fact was true: Lucille Black, based on her own experience, and the difficult relationships she witnessed in her therapy room, no longer believed that marriage could provide happiness.

She would talk to Libby about happiness and marriage. Her own marriage to Libby's father, Morris, had been built on what she had thought was gold but turned out to be straw. Not just his fault, hers as well. The expectations, the thwarted desire, the controlling behaviour, the sabotage. The separation had happened almost a decade earlier but remained an unpleasant memory. Back then, on the day that Lucille was to meet Morris at the lawyer's office, a sudden and fierce thunderstorm, typical on a hot summer day in Winnipeg, produced rain and then more rain, and what care she had taken with her hair that morning became all for nought as she ran from the car to the office. She was late, and she hated being late, and now she was bedraggled and no longer comely. She had worn a black dress that afternoon and was immediately sorry—she wasn't grieving. Everyone else was wearing light fare: summer frocks on the women, short sleeves on the men. Morris, in fact, was wearing shorts, and a ball cap, which lent him such an air of indignity that Lucille felt sorry for him. Until money and the splitting of income was raised, and then all her empathy tumbled into rage.

The thing is, just after their son Martin's death, Morris had imagined that his world was ending and had become reckless with money, cashing in his investments, hiring high-end escorts, offering strangers financial help, and so now he was suffering financially. And Lucille's budgeting and care and thrift would benefit him. She earned more. She had more. They had shared their lives for many years, and it turned out there was a formula for all of this. A formula that one of the lawyers wrote on his iPad and beamed onto a screen. It was all so clear and so logical and so high-tech that there seemed no room for discussion.

She was aghast. She felt erased. She remained calm, though her face was flushed, and she knew that Morris would recognize the symptoms. He'd always laughed at her and said that she couldn't fake a torn heart, not when she was flustered and feeling cornered. A year after Martin's death, just before Lucille left Morris, their marriage in disarray but neither of them willing to admit that disarray, they tried to talk. And failed — because of Lucille's anger, because of Morris's selfishness, because they did not hear each other. And then they decided that they needed to talk about how they would talk. And so, for six months, they had long discussions about words and language and what would enhance their relationship — how something should be said, whether they should just bite their tongues, if Lucille could talk about her sense of betrayal, or if Morris was allowed to use the name of the Minnesota dairy farmer he had fallen for — Ursula — or, God forbid, hold Ursula up as a paragon of goodness.

He had met Ursula online, when she read one of his syndicated columns that he'd written after Martin's death. He was quite popular back then, a columnist who used his deep reading to tap into the anxiety of the regular reader. He received letters from his readers. And one of those readers was Ursula, who had also lost her son in Afghanistan. She was soft-hearted. Generous. Understanding. And she was grieving. According to Morris, everything about Ursula was goodness and light. He told Lucille all of this, as if by confessing he would receive

Lucille's blessing, or absolution. Lucille listened to him and tried to be rational, knowing that Morris was suffering, but she was also suffering, and she hadn't been messy like him and run off into the arms of another lover. She had believed that her marriage was salvageable. Until Morris drove south to Minneapolis to visit Ursula, to meet up and do who knew what with her.

When he returned, she asked him if they'd had sex.

We did not, Morris said.

Did you kiss?

Yes.

How many times?

Does that matter?

It matters in every way. Why didn't you have sex?

It was difficult. I was too sad.

Unbelievable. You've never been too sad to have sex.

You don't know me.

I do. And I don't care about the sex. I'd rather you fuck that woman than talk to her. It's the talking that devastates me. You know why? Because if you're talking to her, it means you're not talking to me.

I'd talk. But you turn away.

I turn away because you always have your head in her lap, your face on her computer.

That was when Morris revealed that he resented Lucille making more money than him, and he resented her parsimony with everything, sex included, and Lucille said that she couldn't fake desire, and Morris went silent.

It was Lucille who left Morris. Their daughters blamed

her for a time, saw Morris as the victim, and she let them believe that. Said nothing to defend herself.

At the lawyer's office, on that rainy day eight years earlier, Lucille's heart had been breaking for her money, which would be ripped from her. She cherished her bank balance, she loved her investments, and she was, she knew, too covetous of lucre. She had shuttered her money away in various forms and myriad places in order to safeguard against financial doom. She would not end up like her father, who had lost everything in a single day. The possibility of being poor, without money, not being able to support herself — these were the reasons she had been so careful to save. And now, here she was, sitting across from Morris and discussing finances, and there was nothing worse in this situation than being the one with everything.

And then Morris's lawyer began talking about Lucille's MedCorp, and the precision and coldness left Lucille stunned. There was no exit. She would have to write Morris a cheque for a large amount. Who said that you couldn't have your cake and eat it too? Morris could. She wanted to ask about the cost of his various women, and the Jaguar that he'd bought, but she didn't, because she was ashamed. Of herself. Of the choices she had made in life. The most telling choice being her marriage to Morris Schutt. And so, she remained quiet.

But not completely quiet, for she phoned her lawyer that evening.

That was a joke, she said. What about pain and suffering? What about betrayal?

The lawyer said that it was impossible to measure pain and suffering.

What about him throwing money around? Lucille asked. I'm on the hook for his hookers? Why didn't we put that on the ledger?

You didn't raise it in the meeting, her lawyer said. But we can certainly discuss that.

Would *you* want to discuss it? Would *you* drag your humiliation into the room and have everyone cut it up and study it? I had no desire. Listen, I know I'm not rational. I know I have to pay. I just wish that he would suffer a little. Everything comes so easily to him. Or if it comes hard, he receives pity.

∞

Two days before she was to leave for Bangkok, a text had come through at five in the afternoon, just as she was sitting down on the deck with a glass of wine. One ping, and then another. She lifted her phone. It was Libby.

feeling pretty bummed out here
fuck my life

                                 Is there something going on?

no, im just sad and confused
even though i have the work here and
what we're doing is good and Shane
im so fucking confused

                                 Aww, I'm sorry, Libby.
                                 Can you talk to someone?

no one
whatever
i have to get up
im in charge of breakfast
Shame talked with me last night
that was good
Shane^

17

what do you think about marriage
mama?
im not sure i believe in it

> I was married. To your father.
> I think it's wonderful that you're asking
> questions.
> Why are you talking about marriage?
> Is he dangerous?

i know!!!! where is dad now?
jesus, mom no! im bigger than him

> There are other dangers besides size.

i feel so alone

> You're strong. You'll be finesse.
> Oops. Fine.

ha
i miss your laugh
your voice

> I met your baby brother.

really? how was that hard?

> Okay. Very beautiful. Jill seems lovely.

dads so childish
he doesn't leave any space for anyone i
don't even have a baby yet and hes on
his second family

she's my age? hesus

jesus^

i talked to dad last week
he said i should do what i want said that
this is what he had learned in life
do what you want

only i don't know what i want

Shane has the most beautiful voice

                        Yeah? He said that?

a little bit of a lisp
and his eyes are so warm
brown warm and soft
his fingers are long very tender
he is so calm
his background is philosophy
lots of metaphors and ideas

                        It sounds like you really like him.

some of the people here

the other workers are very timid

does it? i don't know i think i do

don't be shocked when you see me

the girls all wear jean dresses here

they come down to our ankles and up to

our collar bones

really really really ugly

modest and terribly hot

id like to go to the beach with you and

wear a sarong and a bathing suit and

drink smoothies and eat bacon and eggs

        Thanks for the warning.

        About the dress.

        Do you need anything from here?

tampons

i can't afford them

        Do you like these people, Libby?

and some underwear

calvin klein thongs

        I'd be happy to go to a beach with you.

maybe a bra

white
though everything goes grey in the wash
maybe black and black underwear

no not really

Shane i like
really really really

going to cook now
porridge
or rice
or maybe buy soup

                           Okay. Bye. Love you.

me too

∞

Just before she left for Paris and Thailand, Lucille had spent a weekend by herself at her friend Sally's cottage on Rainy Lake. The cottage was on a small island. She had never come by herself before, and now here she was, all alone. She had to load the boat by the mainland, and start the 9.9 Evinrude, and steer the boat across the lake, and dock it without crashing, and then she had to offload her gear and the groceries, and at night she lay in bed and listened to the night sounds, and the wind soughed and whistled, and it rained furiously one morning, early, and she ran through the rain to the outhouse, and when she returned, she was soaking wet, and she removed her clothes by the door and stood naked and watched the rain fall. There was no one to see her.

She swam around the island three or four times during the day, and at some point, perhaps after the night of the storm, she took to swimming naked, her body moving beneath the water, and she loved it, the freedom, the knowledge of herself, the abandonment. She discovered a mother duck and her brood of seven living in the rushes on the far side of the island. She gave them wide berth, and even so, the mother duck tried to distract Lucille, and flew across the water close to Lucille's head, and then flew in the opposite direction of the nest.

It was during one of her afternoon swims, coming around the outcropping of rock on the east edge of the island, doing her regular and slow breaststroke, when Lucille recalled with utter clarity the day on China Beach when she had nearly lost three-fifths of the family. Perhaps it was the effortlessness of her swimming. Perhaps it was the awareness of the science of floating. But at that moment, she thought of the waves, and the beach, and of Morris, who had saved their daughters.

They'd flown to Vietnam on a family vacation when their three children were much younger — Meredith had been ten, Martin eight, Libby six. They ended up for a few days in Da Nang, staying at a guesthouse near China Beach. They ate seafood, they lolled on the sand, they watched the fishermen in their basket boats set out to sea. Always, after breakfast, the family headed down to the beach. The surf was rough, the waves were wild, and though there was a family rule that the children could not go past the level of their knees, one particular day Morris entered the water and called out to Libby and Meredith to follow him. And they obeyed. Lucille was on the shore with Martin. They were sitting on towels, Martin was digging in the sand, and she was reading. She looked up when she heard Morris call the girls, and immediately she felt anxious, for the waves were mad, and just the day before, an Australian couple had warned the family about riptides. At some point, as she watched with increasing panic, she saw Morris floundering. He was trying to throw the children back to the shore, and then the three of them went under, and they bobbed up

again and were dragged out to sea. And they were gone.
It was as if a rubber band had snapped all three of them
up and dragged them out of sight with terrific speed. She
believed in that moment that they had drowned. And she
imagined going back to Canada with Martin, just the two
of them, and she knew with absolute certainty that she had
lost her husband and her two daughters. She looked around
for help. She ran over to the fishermen, and she yelled and
gestured out at the ocean, and when the men finally understood, they began to push a basket boat out into the water,
fighting the surf. But it was too late. Certainly. She waited,
she looked out into the distance, over the brown, raging
water. And then, far in the distance, down the beach, she
heard a shout, and Lucille saw Morris and Meredith and
Libby walking towards them, and Morris was clutching both
girls, one on each side of him. When they reached Lucille,
she said, You were gone. I thought you had drowned.

The girls had sand in their hair, and Libby had a bruise
on her arm where Morris had gripped her, and Meredith
was quiet, her blue eyes now paler, as if the water or the
sand or the waves had washed the colour away.

The family sat for a time on the beach, no one talking,
and then they gathered up their bags and towels and made
their way slowly back to the guesthouse. That evening, after
the children were sleeping, Morris and Lucille drank a glass
of wine on the patio looking out onto the beach. Lucille
said that it had been a miracle. You were gone, and then
you came back.

I was waving, Morris said. Did you see me?

I saw nothing.

I waved, so that you could locate us. But each time I waved, I had to release Meredith, and I realized that I might lose her, so I stopped waving. The surf kept crashing over our heads, and Libby was crying that we would drown, and I said that no no all was good, though I didn't believe it, but the amazing thing was I had no fear. It was all in the moment. Stay afloat. Don't panic. And then my feet felt sand, and I saw that we had been dragged out and over and back in with the surf, and that's how we ended up way down the beach. That was a marvel. To be desperately struggling to stay afloat, kicking and kicking, and then finding solid ground, and walking up out of the surf holding my two children.

Oh, Morris. I'm so glad it was you. I couldn't have.

You would have, Lucille. It's amazing what you can do when the moment demands it.

My brain would have gone white, and I would have frozen. I know this. And so, I'm glad it was you.

She was glad. And she was grateful. And she was astonished. Morris was a hero.

And now, years later, here was Lucille, in the water, swimming around the island on Rainy Lake, overwhelmed with gratitude and amazement. She knew once again that she could not have done what Morris had done. She was still convinced that she would have panicked. She was not the kind of person who maintained control in the face of potential tragedy. Even though she knew how to swim better than Morris, even though she was strong, she would have fallen short.

Just as she felt she was falling short these days, not thinking clearly, awake at night full of worry.

In a recent session with her own psychiatrist, Dr. Helguson, Lucille had announced that she was going to Thailand to try to convince Libby to leave the little club she had joined.

Dr. Helguson asked why she called it a little club. Is that how you see it? At first it was a cult. Now it's a club.

I don't know what it is. I guess I'll find out.

Did you ever think it might be disrespectful to go there? To insert yourself in Libby's life?

I have. And it is true. But I am still going.

How old is she?

Obviously not old enough to make wise choices.

Why not let her fail? Why not let her choose and see what happens?

When a child wants to climb out on a tree limb that is weak, we don't encourage them. We warn them.

A child, yes. But Libby is her own person. She is not a child.

She acts like a child. She thinks like a child. That makes her a child.

You are still desperately holding the door closed.

Am I? Where is Libby? On this side of the door or the other? I've worked so hard. I've made great leaps. I was so calm after Martin died. I was measured. I gave the right responses. I was in control. People, Morris included, noted how strong I was, how level. But these days, I can't imagine losing another child, my daughter, and my mind flies off somewhere. I'm not losing control in a public way, not yet, but inside, I am terrified. That I might do something irrevocable. I don't want to be crazy.

Of course you are terrified, as you say, that you will do the wrong thing, something irrevocable. You can choose to go to Libby. To see her. She might welcome you. She might tell you to leave. You can be curious. You can ask questions. She might have answers. Or your questions might make her wonder why she doesn't have the answers. You don't know what will happen.

∞

In the years after Martin died, for several summers in a row, she found herself driving out to the soccer complex to watch young men play. She stood at the edge of the bleachers, slightly hidden, holding a cup of coffee, posing as a regular mother, and she watched the players run and call out. Their legs, especially the knees, so vulnerable and beautifully shaped. She wondered what she was doing, hiding in the shade of the bleachers, ogling young men. She told no one about this, as if fearful that, in revealing herself, she might lose herself, which she knew was nonsense, but she liked the feeling of her hidden life — like the notes she wrote to herself as a teenager, confessions, and then pushing them into a hole in the wall behind her bed. And taking them out now and again to recall what she had been thinking at this and that time. And not being so much surprised, but more cognizant that her thinking was not so strange or unusual.

When she thought of Martin, which was always and always, she sometimes fell into self-doubt, and her own failure — that she had spurned Martin, that she had been selfish, that she had overindulged him, that she had underfed him, that she had not protected him from Morris, who had shouted at Martin in a moment of rage, when Martin was eighteen years old, to "go join the fucking army." And Martin had joined the army. Which was so against every idea he had been raised with: a pacifist father, a mother who believed that talking, not violence, was the way to understanding. And yet, the boy had been so happy, toting his kit, cleaning his gun, talking war. And then dying the ignominious death that was labelled friendly fire.

For reasons that she did not quite understand at the time, she agreed to meet the boy who killed Martin. Tyler Goodhand. Poor boy with the unfortunate last name. A year after Martin's memorial service, Tyler made contact with her, and at first she ignored him, but after the second and third letter, she wrote him back, and then a correspondence began, and eventually she agreed to meet with him. She drove up to Shilo to see Tyler in person. Through the wooded glades and rolling hills that flanked the Trans-Canada, a dead deer on the shoulder, crows gathered, and then south to Shilo, where she parked her car, and almost turned around and went home again, but didn't. Tyler had been a mere boy. His small head, the furtive eyes, the obvious wish to cry, but not crying, the soft voice, and these words: I want to apologize, Mrs. Black. I want to say sorry, but I don't know what words to use, there aren't any words to say. Other than, I am sorry.

And she stood and said, Come, and she held him, and then he cried, and she didn't say anything, just held him. And when he was finished crying, they sat across from each other again, and she asked him about his own life, and Tyler said that he was getting married, his girlfriend was pregnant, and he liked fixing up old cars, and then he said that he wanted to go back to Afghanistan. And at that point, she was horrified, but she said nothing. And then they hugged goodbye.

Driving home that day, she called Morris — at that time they still talked — and when he answered, she said that Tyler, the boy who shot Martin, was planning on going back to Afghanistan. I mean, what the fuck, Morris. What — so he can kill some more of his companions?

It makes me sad, Lucille said. And angry. What right does he have to work on his cars, and have a baby, and go back to war, and hold a gun?

I'll talk to someone, Morris said.

No, Morris. Don't. That's not why I called. Tyler's just a young boy. He looks fifteen. It's not his fault that someone gave him a rifle. So don't call anyone. Don't do your soapbox.

Soapbox. Is that how you see it?

No. But you do.

You were never sad enough, Lucille. That was the problem. It wasn't Martin's death that separated us, it was your lack of grief.

We've talked about this, Morris. There wasn't enough room for both of us to be wailing in public. You took up all the space, left me nowhere to go. No place to be sad.

Did I? Oh.

Yes.

I still do that?

Doesn't matter. We're not living together.

Do you want to? Get back together?

No, Lucille said. It never works for couples to climb

back onto a wagon that's heading pell-mell down the hill. No turning it around.

Why'd you go see him? Morris asked. Whatever could it help?

I was looking for our son, Lucille said. Some detail. Something I might have not known about him. But I see now that I do know him. Knew him. Everything that was important. Did I ever tell you about the time we were chased by the beet-faced man in the red pickup?

And then, not waiting for an answer, she began to talk.

Martin was driving, I was playing front-seat driver. He was sixteen. Just new to the road. At a red light, Martin forgets to put on his left-turn signal and then does so at the last moment. He says, Ooops. There's a long blast from a horn, and it's a guy behind us in a red pickup. Martin makes a cautious left turn, and then notices that the pickup has decided to follow us. Right on our bumper. And Martin gets frightened. He picks up speed. I look back. The pickup is still there. The man is florid, and that's scary. Big temper. His mouth is moving, he's yelling at us. I tell Martin to pull over and let him pass. And so, Martin does. Pulls over to the curb. But the man doesn't go around us. He sidles up close right beside us and you can see him screaming. He rolls down his passenger window. I'm afraid now. Martin is cowering, poor boy. And then the beet-faced man throws a whole cup of Tim Hortons coffee at us. We are swamped. The car is. And the man drives away. We sit there for a bit and then we look at each other and we start to laugh. And we laugh so hard I'm going to pee my pants. Martin has tears running down his face, he's so relieved and so happy. Jesus, he says. Jesus. What a waste of coffee, he says. And for some reason, that makes us laugh even more. That was Martin. He had no spite. No sense of revenge. Which is why I can't imagine him carrying a rifle. Firing it at someone.

Of course you can't, Morris said.

And then he asked if Lucille was okay.

Fine. I'm okay. I'm sorry to bother you, Morris.

No, no. I like it.

Bye, Morris, she said. And she let him go.

She was passing through the rolling hills east of Shilo. The trees were bright green and the clear sky almost white. She was floating above the ground, and she began to laugh, and she heard him laughing with her, and she laughed until she hiccupped and began to sob, and then, fearing for her life, she pulled over and stopped on the shoulder until her crying was done.

∞

She had planned to take an air-conditioned bus down to Pattaya upon arriving in Bangkok, but the flight was delayed out of Hong Kong, and she arrived late at night, and so decided to take a room at a guesthouse off Silom Road, near the downtown. Exiting the taxi in the *soi* near the entrance to the guesthouse, she saw rats, and she smelled cooking out on the streets, and driving in from the airport the lights of Silom Road had been brilliant, and the sidewalks full of people and vendors had surprised her. No one appeared to sleep in this city.

A friend had recommended the guesthouse for its peace and quiet. And this was true. It was heavily fortified with gates and fences, and the room she occupied gave out onto an interior garden where a man in a blue uniform circled the paths. He was there when she went to sleep, and he was still there when she woke, and for some reason, the constancy of the man in the blue uniform made her anxious. At breakfast, in a family-style dining area, she was seated with a missionary family who worked with the Hmong up north near Chiang Rai. They were six in total. The parents and the four children all appeared to speak Thai with great ease. The children were very well-behaved, and clean, and open-faced. The father said that the country was still celebrating the rescue of the twelve boys and their soccer coach from the caves up north, which was not far

from their home in the highlands. He said that it was a tale
of being lost and then being found, and he said that the
story itself, the despair and then the joy, could be translated
into the plight of everyman. It was a gift, he said, because
the Hmong saw so easily the connection between the cave
rescue and their own need to be guided from the darkness
of their own cave into the light of salvation. He said that
the hill tribe people, being animists, caught on quickly to
the allegories and metaphors of Christianity, in fact many
of their stories shared Christianity's sense of sacrifice. He
shook his head in amazement. His wife was quietly telling
the youngest child, a girl with blond pigtails, to finish her
glass of milk, which she stoically did.

The father said that the rescue was especially fortuitous
for the government, a military junta that had been suffering
in popularity but was now hugely loved. He said that in
a cynical world, this was a good story. The rescuers were
heroes. As were the boys.

The wife asked Lucille what reasons she had for visiting
Thailand, and Lucille wondered why a reason was necessary. She said that she was a tourist.

Later, strolling through the garden, she saw the missionary children playing on the swings, the eldest two pushing
the younger two, and she was aware of the decorum and
the kindness of the older children, and the generosity of
language, and the perfection of behaviour, and she wondered how it was possible to produce children in this
manner. Would these children, in their adolescence and
twenties, fall into disrepair? Rebel? Swing wildly away
from the strictures of their upbringing? Probably not. They

would all be healthy and fine citizens, perhaps even follow in the footsteps of their parents and become savers of souls. And their parents would never suffer the ignominy of their children failing to thrive.

Of course, she had never wanted her children to be obedient. She had encouraged questions and scepticism. The danger, of course, was that too much scepticism would lead to where Libby was today. A blind acceptance of the words of a mountebank and charlatan. Simply because it was easy. Or felt good. In her darkest moments, usually in the middle of the night, wide awake, Lucille created a list detailing everything she had done wrong in the nurturing of her children. Too harsh, too soft, daycare, too much sugar, hovering, breastfed too long or not long enough, poor discipline, poor modelling, the breakup with Morris, taking the heart surgeon as a lover, not pushing her children hard enough, giving up on music lessons for them, working late, swearing in front of them, showing anger, fighting with Morris, berating Morris in front of them, being too acquiescent in her marriage. All true, and not true. And in the light of day, dismissed as fearful and irrational reasoning.

Ever since that barrage of texts, Libby had gone silent. Even when Lucille had sent Libby a short text announcing her arrival in Bangkok, there had been no response. Which was typical for Libby. She had spilled her anguish onto Lucille, and now she felt better. Which was worrying. Lucille didn't want Libby to feel better. She wanted her to think.

Earlier, Libby had given the address in Pattaya where the compound was located. Very simple: Take an aircon, a blue bus, from the main station on Sukhumvit, and get off at the station in Pattaya. From there, take a tuk-tuk to this address. A five-minute ride. Ring the bell on the outside wall. Someone will come.

And someone did come. A young woman in a light-coloured jean dress that covered her entire body. Blond hair, a long braid, a flat, open face. Her name was Carol. She shook Lucille's hand and lifted her bag and led her towards the main house, saying that everyone was expecting Lucille. It was wonderful when parents came to visit. She hoped that Lucille would stay for some time and share the vision of the group. Libby was at the market right then, shopping for the evening meal. The others were in the classroom. Everyone had a job. Carol's job on that particular day was to be the greeter. She said that there were occasions when a stranger might come, curious about the project, and what had been at first simple inquisitiveness turned into a full-fledged commitment to the group. Carol said that this was the influence of Shane, whose vision was infectious. She said that he had an amazing capacity to make every person feel special.

Carol might have been in her early twenties, but the braid, and her lack of makeup, and her guilelessness, gave the impression that she was a teenager wearing an old woman's dress.

Lucille was guided past a kitchen where three girls who all looked like Carol were peeling potatoes. They looked up as Carol led Lucille towards her bedroom, but they did not speak, and Carol did not offer introductions. The girls were whispering together.

Carol opened a door and stepped into a small room. Lucille followed. A single bed. A thin sheet on the bed. A small, square pillow. An overhead fan. A broomstick for a clothes hanger. This was the room she would be staying in. Carol placed Lucille's suitcase on the bed, stepped backwards out of the room, and just before she closed the door, she said, Make yourself at home.

Lucille sat on the hard bed. She touched the square pillow. Her chest was tight, her breathing shallow. Sweat ran between her breasts. She turned on the overhead fan and discovered that it had one speed, very fast, with an extreme wobble, and out of fear that it would drop and chop off her head, she turned it off. She heard voices in the hallway, and she stood, anticipating company, perhaps Libby, but the voices faded away.

She wondered if she was allowed to open the door.

∞

An hour later, she was dragging her suitcase through the streets of Pattaya. Alone. Before leaving the compound, she had sat for a time on the single bed in the bare room and then she'd left the room and wandered the hallways of the large house. In a separate hut, away from the house, she had come across two Thai women bent over an exercise book. One of the women was counting in English. Lucille looked in, was not noticed, and walked on. In the yard, a young woman was feeding a toddler, following her around, slipping a spoonful of rice into the child's mouth, and then continuing the amble across the compound, zigzagging, no concerns, the chatter of Thai, the enormous heat. Lucille stood in the shade of an awning and watched. She returned to her room, waited some more, and then took her suitcase and trundled it to the front gate and out onto the street. She was soaked with sweat by the time she found a room in a small hotel, on the second floor, with a patio that gave onto the glimmering pool below. There was air conditioning, and there was a mini-bar, and the bed was firm, and the bathroom was clean, and the pillows were soft and not square.

She texted Libby and gave her the hotel name and the room number. And then she changed into her bathing suit and went down to the pool below and settled onto a chaise longue. She ordered a Kloster, and when it came, she poured the beer into the cold glass that had come with it, and she drank and set the glass down on the small table beside her and she closed her eyes.

That night, she ate pad Thai at a restaurant near her hotel. She drank bottled water. She was still alone. She had logged into the wifi at the restaurant, and she kept checking her phone. Nothing.

She left the restaurant and walked towards the beach area. Darkness, even though it was only eight in the evening. The tide was out and there were shapes of people down on the beach, stooping to gather objects. Crabs perhaps. She went back up towards Walking Street and was met by the sound of music and bars and lights and hawkers selling watches and T-shirts and belts. She was asked if she wanted a boy, or a girl. She turned away. There were tourists, many of them Europeans, and many of them men, who walked in large groups and took up space. She avoided them by slipping sideways as they approached. They did not see her at all. They were looking for something else.

Back at her hotel, she sat in her dress and sandals by the pool and ordered a glass of white wine, which was too sweet and too warm. She drank it anyway. A young couple sat nearby, eating, speaking English, and then another language, perhaps Thai, she could not know, and then back to English. The fluency and effortlessness lulled her. She heard their voices, and she heard the sounds of their spoons touching the bowls and plates, and their exclamations at the spiciness of the food. Their voices came at her in waves,

inconsequential, very small in contrast to the vastness of
the sky above her, and the vastness of the emptiness inside
her.

Sometime after Martin died, perhaps a year later, Lucille
found that her thinking was disconnected. She had dealt
with clients who experienced dissociation, particularly as
a reaction to trauma, and so she knew the signs and the
dangers. She confessed to her psychiatrist that she was
terrified of what was happening to her.

I'm all over the place, she said. I am standing in a wheat
field and a crop-duster keeps buzzing me, and at some
point the crop-duster takes off my head. Just like that, my
head is gone. And then I'm eight years old, and I'm visiting
a friend named Kimmy, and we are running naked through
a house after a bath, and Kimmy's father is there telling
us to run faster so we might dry off. He is sitting in a chair
and cheering us on. It is an old schoolhouse and there are
children's desks and blackboards, and on the blackboards,
someone has drawn pictures of chickens without heads.
And then my mother with her back to me, looking over
her shoulder, and I feel so much love for my mother that I
fear I will not be able to breathe. And then Morris's mouth
moving, telling me that Martin is dead. And there are times
when I think Martin is still alive, and I even pick up the
phone to talk to him, and only when I hear that the number
is not in service do I understand that he is dead. I don't
know what to do.

Silence in the room. And then Dr. Helguson asked her if she was able to sleep.

Some, Lucille said. But I wake from nightmares, and I am afraid to go back to sleep. I should write the dreams down, I know, but it would be like reliving the nightmare. And so, I imagine being held by my mother. Back when I was young, she did the best she could. She was sick, as you know, and she was in the hospital for a time, but when she came home, I was delirious with gratitude, and did everything to keep her from leaving again.

And so, you are afraid. That you will be left again. That you will be alone.

I *am* alone. Completely.

But you are here. Talking to me. What about your daughters? Your grandson? Do you have conversations?

Yes. But when I am alone again, I am exhausted, simply because I had to work so hard not to sound crazy. The other day my daughter Meredith and I were talking about a recipe, and I told her that Martin had it, she should ask him, and of course she reminded me that Martin was dead. Meredith thinks that I am going nuts. I think that.

We have talked about it. Should we again talk about how he died?

Lucille shook her head. I'm okay, she said. And she began to cry. Oh shit, she said through her tears, I told myself I wouldn't cry. She wiped at her face with the back of her hand. She waited. Closed her eyes. She opened her eyes and she put a fist against her chest and said, I can feel it way inside me. It's like I have a cave there and it goes deep. I didn't know that it was possible to have that much space there. So much space. And so deep. I do not think it will go away.

You are very clear right now, Dr. Helguson said. That is good. I see no problem with your mind.

I hate November eleventh, Lucille said. I hate people who wear poppies. I want to go up to them and ask what right they have, wearing that thing.

It is personal.

And illogical.

Is it possible that you have earned the right?

But I don't want to have earned it. I want nothing like that. I want to go back.

Of course you do, Dr. Helguson said.

But I can't, Lucille said. She folded her hands and held them in her lap and looked down at them.

When she was sixteen years old, Lucille's father offered to take her to Tanzania to climb Mount Kilimanjaro. She wasn't interested in the mountain, but she didn't see much of her father at that time, he was invested in the business of being busy, and she thought that if she said yes and went to Tanzania with him, they would become closer. Her mother, who didn't like the idea of the mountain or the possible danger, was worried. But her mother's worrying made Lucille even happier about her choice. At that age, anything to displease her mother was pleasing to Lucille.

The night before the climb, she and her father went for dinner at a small restaurant next to their hotel in Moshi. A young German couple dined beside them. The German couple said that they would be climbing the next day as well, and so Lucille's father and the German couple talked about routes and guides and altitude sickness while Lucille listened to the German manner of putting English sentences together. She was particularly interested in Eva, the woman, who gave off an aura of aloofness and scepticism, which led Lucille to considering her own life, and what she would be like when she grew up. Not aloof, she hoped. She knew that it was odd to be using language like *when she grew up*, for she already saw herself in some ways as grown up, but she also sensed that she had much to learn.

She and her father began the climb early in the morning. It was well into the third day, halfway up the mountain, that Lucille became sick. She threw up that evening, and her father and the guide decided that her father would continue climbing, and Lucille would return to Moshi. There was a group heading down after a successful climb, and she joined that group, walking slowly, having trouble breathing, while her father continued his ascent. Back at her hotel, she slept and ate and slept. She drank lots of water.

The morning after her descent, she met Rolf, the German, in the restaurant. He too had gotten altitude sickness, and he had returned to Moshi while his wife continued to the peak. Rolf was ashamed to admit his failure. He said those words: I'm ashamed. Lucille hadn't felt shame at all. She was relieved. But then she wondered if she even knew what shame felt like. Or if she had ever experienced it. Perhaps only adults suffered shame. She did not know. And so, she wondered about the word *shame*, and what it meant to Rolf, and she wondered why she didn't feel the same. She spent the next few days with Rolf, while they waited for her father and Eva to reappear. They ate together, they played checkers in the evening, they explored Moshi, though it was a small town and after one full day of walking they had exhausted the sights.

They talked. Rolf asked her questions about herself and her family and she did not reveal much, other than to talk about her sister and her brothers and to speak of her mother, whom she missed, being so far from her. She told Rolf nothing about having wanted to run from her mother. Her feelings confused her. Rolf began to speak of himself and his wife. Out of the blue, he said that Eva suffered depression sometimes. When Rolf said the word *depression*, he said it in German, and it took a few seconds for Lucille to understand the word, even though it was very close to English. Rolf said that it was difficult. It made him angry, which was ridiculous, and it made him sad. He said that long ago, before he married Eva, and when he already knew of Eva's difficulties, his mother had told him to run. He had not listened. And now he could not run, for he and Eva were completely entangled. He said that this trip to Kilimanjaro was to be a form of therapy for Eva. A doctor had told her that climbing a mountain might be a cure, and so they had done some research and come up with a walking mountain, this one. Rolf said that it was ironic that he was the one who had failed, and Eva was up on top of the mountain. He said that she had learned how to breathe without much oxygen long ago, and this was something that he had not learned.

On the third evening after her return from the mountain, Lucille sat in the hotel dining room waiting for Rolf to appear. They had not arranged to meet, but because they had eaten together the previous two evenings, she assumed that he would once again appear. She found herself choosing her clothes carefully before meeting him, aware that he was aware of her. She was youthful, and she had a certain beauty, she knew this, but she hadn't experienced her own presence in the way she had over the last few evenings with Rolf. She had no designs. She was just conscious of a feeling and an admiration, and she felt safe with Rolf, for he was a complete gentleman. When she was to think about it later, as an older woman, she realized that she had felt powerful and in control, and that she had been seducing herself, a form of self-confidence and flattery that would that evening, in one glance, be shattered.

She waited for an hour in the restaurant, and when Rolf did not appear, she ordered a small plate of fries and a Coke, and when she was finished, she signed the bill and left the restaurant. The hotel bar adjoined the restaurant, and she had to pass by it on her way back to the staircase that led to her room. In passing, she glanced inside and saw Rolf sitting at the bar with a woman, young and certainly local. The two of them were talking intimately and the woman was touching Rolf's shoulder and he was holding her hand, which rested on the bar. Lucille turned away. She felt as if she had been caught doing something wrong. She worried that Rolf had seen her.

She decided then that she would walk out into the night. Rolf had advised her not to go out on her own. It was dangerous. She kept to the lighted streets, and then she slipped sideways down a small lane and found herself in a park. She sat on a metal bench. She was alone, and it was very quiet. There were no street lights. Out of the darkness, quite unexpectedly, a man appeared. He stood before her and asked her name. She said that she was a tourist. She stood to leave, and the man blocked her way. He said that she had beautiful hair. Yes, he said. She stepped sideways and walked away. She did not turn when he called after her. She was shaking, and then she began to run. She found herself on a larger street where there were a few pedestrians. She slowed down, but she still didn't look back, as if that would invite danger. Back in her room, she sat on her bed, and then finally she climbed into the bed fully clothed, regretting what she now knew. Though she couldn't have said what she now knew. There was something else that she felt. It might be jealousy. Or envy. Maybe sadness. For herself? She couldn't say. She wanted to go home and get back to her own life. She decided that she would no longer try to please her father, who was at that moment high on a mountain, doing exactly as he pleased.

Her father and Eva returned to Moshi the following afternoon. They were ecstatic, and when the four of them had supper together that evening, her father and Eva regaled Rolf and Lucille with the exhilaration of the summit. Rolf was quiet. As was Lucille. She did not look at Rolf. She sat and watched Eva talk and talk, and she watched her father watch Eva talk, and she saw that they were both very happy, and this made her sad, for whereas she had originally believed that Eva might be stupid and naive, Lucille saw that the adult world was imprudent and driven by selfishness and that maybe she was the naive one.

At night, somewhere near her Pattaya hotel, a rooster crowed, its internal clock apparently off. The sun rose at six. She sat up, slipped into her bathing suit, smelled rice cooking, and was immediately hungry. She had not slept well, waking at two in the morning, cold from the air conditioner, rising to turn it off, opening a window, lying down again, pushing back her thoughts, and then acquiescing and being overwhelmed by memories — the fabric of her mind. She breathed slowly and deeply. She missed her mother. She missed Meredith and Jake. She had always suffered from homesickness, in fact had been astounded at the deep ache she felt for home every time she travelled, though she hid it well, swallowed the nausea, and ploughed ahead.

She had planned to spend ten days in Pattaya, visiting with Libby, going to the beach, exploring, but she already knew that none of this would happen. For one, the beach was dirty and no one was swimming. Also, the city was loud and vulgar and driven by male desire. She had stopped at a travel agency the previous day and found that she might fly to Phuket, over on the other side of the gulf, and from there take a boat to a small island called Phi Phi, which, because it was not the tourist season and because of the monsoons and rains, would have lots of rooms to let.

After swimming fifty laps, she sat by the pool and ate noodle soup and drank ice coffee. She was alone. Her phone was silent. Her head was quieter. Someone somewhere was playing tinny music in a language she did not understand. The soup was hot, and when she was finished, she was sweating. She dipped back into the pool and floated on her back. She heard voices, muffled by the water. When she raised her head, she saw the same couple who had been eating poolside the evening before. They were standing at the edge of the pool, and the woman was talking quickly in English and she was looking down at the man, for he was shorter and his head was bowed. He said something, which might have been Thai. Again, Lucille did not know. The woman's hands chopped the air. She said, Don't speak. Just don't speak. And then she finished speaking and dived into the pool and swam underwater right past Lucille. The woman wore a one-piece that revealed the muscles on her back and the length of her legs. Lucille imagined the couple having sex, the all-out heft of the woman bearing down on the man.

Lucille climbed from the pool and walked to her table and wrapped herself in a towel and sat on a chair. The man was seated now as well, staring off into the distance, across the pool from where Lucille was sitting. Lucille could not help watching him, for they were opposite each other, though separated by water. The man was not at all aware of her, nor was the woman, who had climbed from the pool, water dripping off her, and gone to the man and sat and then called out to the waiter by the bar. She spoke in the same language that the man had spoken earlier. Then the woman picked up a towel and laid it over her lap and she pushed her hair back over her shoulders, dried her hands, and folded them in her lap. She began to speak in his language. She was very fluent, and she talked and talked. The man stared off into the distance and did not speak. At some point, the waiter delivered ice coffee to the woman, who leaned forward and stirred the coffee with a spoon, and then drank. And it was only when she sipped her coffee that she stopped speaking. In that pause, the man lit a cigarette. He said a few words, and this set the woman off on another soliloquy. There was something effortless in the man's acceptance of the woman's speech. Either he'd heard this all before, or he didn't care, or he knew that it was a necessary thing. His face was impassive. And then the woman stopped speaking. And she began to cry. Which was surprising, because her voice had been so fierce, and she had looked so strong. The man reached out and took the woman's hand.

At this point, Lucille stood and gathered her things and walked up to her room, aware that she had been privy to something that was private. The night before, listening to this same couple, she had been affected by their conversation; not the meaning of the words — she could not understand everything — but the fact that they conversed, that they seemed to have a relationship. But this morning, her perspective had changed. She had now in her head the image of a very different woman, not as strong, not as fierce, angrier, perhaps afraid. Of what, she could not know. She had no idea what caused the tears.

In her room, she removed her bathing suit and showered. She would send Carl a note, tell him that she was enjoying the heat, and the humidity, tell him how her skin was smoother now, and softer, tell him that she had just witnessed a moment between a woman and a man by the pool, tell him that she was so relieved that he didn't frighten her, as men could, tell him that she loved how, when he wanted her, he always asked if it was okay, was she okay, was this okay. How about this? Can I hold you?

Carl was her lover — it was a habit that she saw him every Friday. Always at his condo on Waterfront Drive. Lucille demanded privacy in her relationship with Carl, and he accepted this, though he sometimes wished for more. She understood this but made it clear that she wasn't ready to make their relationship public. She liked him, but she didn't love him. He was convenient. He was a fine enough lover, an older man who required some patience and coaxing, but she didn't mind. She liked his cleanliness, the organization of his spice rack, the immaculateness of his closets, all his shirts neatly hung, his shoes lined up, the art on his walls, his baroque music collection. Every Friday, they ate a meal together, perhaps watched something on Netflix, or sat on his balcony that overlooked the river, and then they went inside and undressed and had a drink as they talked, and then they made love. She knew her body. She knew that though she felt little desire for Carl before they had sex, the feelings would arrive during the sex, and those feelings never failed her. This was what it meant to be her age. He liked to watch her walk naked around his condo. And she obliged, which surprised her sometimes, because she had always been a bit shy with Morris, perhaps because Morris had been too aggressive, and Carl was anything but aggressive. He loved her body, and he said so in a soft and non-sexual way, if that was possible, and he liked to take photos of her, both clothed and naked, which was certainly sexual, and this too Lucille allowed with great equanimity, though she made Carl promise that the photos would remain private. And he agreed. However, she was not foolish. She knew the possibilities of betrayal, and the potential danger of the photos being shared, but she did not care for some reason, though *not caring* was a form of looseness that might mean that she cared a lot. Perhaps she liked the risk. She had met Carl online, which had also been a surprise, for her experience of meeting men online had not been good. But when she found Carl, she knew right away that he was safe — and so she chose him because he was safe. The couple by the pool — which was how Lucille now designated them — were a reflection of Lucille and Carl. The submission. The ambivalence. The seeking. The apology. Oh, to be clear, Lucille was not that woman. But perhaps Carl was that man in some way.

On the Friday just before her trip, Carl had convinced her to ride out to Patricia, a windswept, unkempt beach on Lake Winnipeg that was popular on weekends, but during the week very few people came, and so they would have privacy. They set up an umbrella and laid out their towels, and just as she stretched out with her book, she saw her brother Will walking along the shoreline, heading in the direction of the nude beach. He was alone, dragging a cooler behind him, a towel slung over his shoulder. Lucille had been lying on her stomach, looking out to the brown water of the lake, watching the gulls dive, her chin resting on her hands, when she saw him. She didn't call out. She didn't say anything. She might have if she'd been alone, but she wasn't. She was with Carl, and she hadn't wanted Will to meet Carl, or Carl to come face to face with Will. It was too layered, and too open to misinterpretation and conjecture.

Will was her youngest sibling. She had a much older sister, Val, who lived in South America and visited every three years. And there was Harv, who lived in Vancouver, and who flew in twice a year to see their mother. He would take care of Mother with a ferocious intensity, paying rapt attention and telling his siblings what a wonderful thing it was to take care of Mother, and then, within two days, he was exhausted. And the rest of the time he avoided his mother, and went out with friends, complained about their mother, and went home. This was the brother who could not stop talking, the one who, when he asked someone a question, which was rare, was already formulating his own story while the answer to his question was being given. He was not attuned to subtlety.

And then there was Will, a middle-aged man who had never truly grown up. He lived by himself in a small house on Euclid in the north end. He was unemployed. Certainly not thin. Ate poorly. Played in a blues band. He rode an electric bicycle around the city, and so it was that on his bicycle, as in life, he never had to pedal. He was terrified of death and sickness. And he was the happiest person Lucille had ever known. Everyone loved Will. He ate lunches with their mother every weekday, not because he necessarily wanted to spend time with his mother, but because he could eat for free. Their mother worried about him, but Will had a convincing manner, and he managed to persuade his mother that his life was a good one, even though he didn't have a job, or money. He was, in fact, the best kind of son. He did not look down on his mother. He did not try to control her. Rather than spending time, as Lucille inevitably did, cleaning their mother's apartment, organizing her pills, calling home care, tidying up the Depends lying everywhere, and washing dishes, he would sit with his mother and tell her interesting stories from his life, and he would eat his free meals, and then he would depart. Will had always looked out for himself. And not looked out for himself. Their mother adored him. He could do no wrong.

A month before she went on her trip, suddenly panicked about her mother, who would need some attention while Lucille was gone, she had left a message for Will. She told him that she would be out of the country, and he would need to take over for a while. When he called back, he said that he would look in on their mother. No problem. He might even take her out to McDonald's one day for lunch. She needed to get out of that place once in a while, have some fun. Get some air.

Lucille said that their mother had a hair appointment on Saturday, and a doctor's appointment on Tuesday. Also, her good friend Leona was quite ill and if she died while Lucille was gone, there would be a funeral.

No way I do funerals, Will said. Haircut, maybe. Also, I don't do doctor's appointments. You know that.

Just drop her off at the door to the clinic. Can you manage that?

What if she gets lost?

You'll find her, Will. She won't die. And make sure her teeth are in. She likes to put them in her jacket pocket, or in the garbage. She's already lost a set.

Jesus, Lucille. You must get so tired. How can you stand it?

What he meant was, How can you stand being you? But she ignored this. If she truly confronted herself, she feared that she might agree with her brother. How could she stand being her? But if she wasn't her, then who would be her? How would anything get done?

On the day at the beach, Carl was photographing Lucille lying on the sand in her bathing suit, a black tankini, which was flattering. Carl had said so. She didn't trust that he was telling the truth, and yet she wanted to believe that she might look okay. To him. He was squatting with his back to the lake, his face blocked out by the camera, when she saw Will in the distance. She lifted her hand and waved Carl away. He was surprised, but he lowered the camera and came and lay down beside her.

He touched her hair, ran his hand along her back, and asked if she was okay.

She said that all was fine. She said that she wanted to go soon. Okay?

He said sure. Any time.

She thought of her brother stripping down on the beach just around the bend. Pushed that image away. He had looked so happy, so contented, full of anticipation. Lucille envied this. She wanted some anticipation in her life. For something. For anything. She closed her eyes and perhaps she slept, for when she lifted her head again, Carl was kneeling in the sand, at a distance, playing with his camera.

That evening, she told Carl that she would be gone for a month. She told him where she would be going. He said that he was happy for her. She deserved a holiday. Maybe she would come back relaxed and refreshed. He was too nice. Too gentle. Too generous. She was slightly repulsed by all the niceness. She kissed him on the cheek.

You sweet man, she said.

∞

In the morning, early, she left her hotel and walked over to the compound and rang the bell. No one came. She rang again. And again. She called out. Finally, the lock went back and the gate opened and a young girl, not Carol, but a girl just like Carol, stood before her. She had the sullen face of a child who has just been dragged from her bed.

Lucille said that she was Libby's mother, and she would like to talk to her daughter.

I'll have to ask, the girl said.

You do that. And while you're at it, tell Shane I'd like to see him as well.

Oh, he doesn't usually take visitors this early. My name is Jordanna. She ducked her head shyly, as if by giving her name she had crossed a forbidden boundary.

It's my daughter I want to talk to, Lucille said. Please find her.

Jordanna walked away, leaving Lucille by the gate.

Beneath a tamarind tree, in the yard, there was a single metal chair. Lucille sat down in the shade. She was already sweating, and it was barely eight in the morning. She heard voices. She heard people eating. She heard the chatter of children. But it was all inside the walls somewhere, away from her. She saw no movement.

And then Libby appeared. She came out of a doorway, far back in the compound, and she walked towards Lucille.

She walked slowly, her arms at her side. She was the same, only thinner. Still striking. Her sharp nose, her wide mouth. The dress. She was barefoot.

Mother, she said, and Lucille stood and approached her and hugged her.

Are you okay? Lucille asked.

Of course. I'm so glad to see you.

You didn't answer my texts. I thought you'd been kidnapped.

Libby laughed. She went up on tiptoes and touched Lucille's cheek. She said that there was no wifi. Sometimes yes. Sometimes no.

Lucille said they would go for breakfast now. Libby said that she was just sitting down with the group. Lucille said that she wanted to be alone with her.

Libby seemed afraid. Or maybe she was embarrassed. Of the imposition of her mother, who was throwing a stark reflection onto her existence. It would be difficult. Lucille recognized this. She took Libby by the hand and said that she had no intentions. Only a conversation. I've come all this way, we might as well have breakfast together.

Libby smiled. Your voice is shrill, she said.

I brought your things. What you asked for.

Libby said that she had been in a state, asking for tampons and underwear as if those things might make her happier.

Underwear is underwear, Lucille said. It's not about happiness.

You're still the same, Mom. Aren't you. A materialist.

Really? Was that how she was seen? She, who spent her days weaving through the mind, was a materialist? She'd never heard that word in Libby's mouth before.

I want Shane to come, Libby said.

Lucille said that if this was what Libby truly wanted, of course he could come.

Libby said that she didn't know anymore what she truly wanted.

Lucille sat Libby down on the chair and walked towards the area where she had seen the three girls peeling potatoes the day before. She found a group of women sitting at a long wooden table in the dining room. She asked if they knew where Shane was, and one of the girls pointed towards the kitchen. The other girls offered dark and confused looks.

She found him standing in the kitchen, eating some sort of green sauce mixed in with rice. Lumps of broccoli as well. She didn't know it was him at first, but she did know, because he was alone, and he was in the kitchen, and this was where she had been told he was, and there were no other men in the room, and she had seen a photo of him previously, in which he had been standing with Libby on the beach, and so she knew it was him. In the photo, he had been cleanshaven, and now he had a beard, and this made him look older. Something graceless and forced in his manner. She knew this kind of man. Had seen him in her therapy room. He was usually a talker, and hid his anxiety by feigning a meditative stance. Not a winker, certainly.

More a sleepy, wrinkled, creased smile, and a soft voice, demanding the listener lean forward to catch the words.

She was being too harsh. She didn't know him at all. She approached him and said that she was Libby's mother, and that she would be taking her daughter out for breakfast.

He said of course, and he set down his bowl and reached out a hand.

She took it. He was strong. And did not just touch her palm but held it for a while, and then let go at just the right moment, before discomfort set in. Her discomfort.

I will join you, he said.

Lucille said that it would be just the two of them.

He asked if this was what Libby wanted.

It is what I want, Lucille said.

Shane was leaning against the sink, his arms were crossed, and he was wearing a white T-shirt. He had no hair on his forearms, and they were tanned and muscled and tattooed. Tattoos on his neck as well. Lucille had a theory that tattoos were a cry for attention, an exterior response to an unfilled interior. Libby had said nothing about what Shane was or where he'd come from, and Lucille hadn't asked. It was humid and hot, but he seemed unaffected by the heat. Lucille was sweating. He was smiling, looking her in the eye. His teeth were brilliant. He spoke with a slight lisp, which made him softer and more vulnerable, and this had an appeal.

He said that when Libby first joined the group here, she had been confused and lost. But in the last while, she had blossomed, she was stronger now, she was healthier.

Her face glowed. You must have noticed the difference, Dr. Black.

Lucille had no good answer to these proclamations. She wanted to say, Nonsense, but she only said, Lucille. Please call me Lucille.

What he called her appeared to be of no consequence to him. He was watching Lucille intently, as if she might be a painting on a wall and it was his job to interpret that painting. His eyes didn't leave her. She looked down at her hands as if they might be offering her advice. He said that Lucille and her daughter were isomorphic. He had learned this from talking to Libby, and from their therapy together. And when Lucille walked into the room, he saw it immediately. You have, physically even, the same gait. And internally, you are both independent. Fiercely so. It's fascinating, don't you think, how this works?

Lucille said that they would be back in a while, and she turned and walked away.

In the hallway, the girl at the table who had directed Lucille into the kitchen took her arm and said that Libby had gone back to her room. She kept a hand on her arm and guided her down a hallway to a doorway. As they walked, the girl said that her name was Essie, and she said that she was perceived as one of the rebellious ones in the compound. As was Libby. She said that Shane was most fascinated by the women he couldn't control. She said that she planned to leave. Shane had wanted her, she had rejected him, and now he wanted Libby. Here was her room.

A bare space, and a single bed on which Libby was sitting. Her small backpack, a few clothes hanging from nails, an overhead fan that turned slowly, not a book to be found, no photos. Gone was the girl who had always set up a home wherever she landed, laying out a few special objects, her favourite novel, postcards.

Come, Lucille said. It's all arranged.

∞

They walked through the streets of Pattaya. The street cleaners were out, pushing away with their brooms the detritus of the night before. They walked hand in hand. It was Libby who had taken her hand and refused to let go. They found a café that served cappuccinos and pastries.

Libby ate her croissant quickly, and then ate the remainder of Lucille's croissant.

Do you get enough to eat? Lucille asked.

Oh, yes. Lots. Too much. Shane thinks that overeating is an offence.

What about just eating? Is that an offence?

No. Of course not. He does like us thin, though.

And you? What do you like?

I don't have to try. The heat just eats the pounds off of me.

I can see.

I'm happy, Mama.

Where does he get his money?

There are donors. They see the work as valuable. It is valuable.

What is the work?

We teach English to the young women who work in the sex clubs. And we teach sewing so that they can get better work in the factories.

You don't sew, Lucille said. Her voice felt strained, pushy.

You're right. But I speak English.

And Shane does therapy? Lucille asked. Her tone was falsely soft this time.

He does. He's very quick, like you. With his words. He's constantly catching me out, challenging my thinking.

Lucille said nothing.

I know that you think I'm crazy, Libby said. You see this as a cult. It isn't. We're all free to come and go. I could leave tomorrow.

Do you want to leave?

Oh. No. She said this with a whisper and then began to cry. And when she was finished crying, and had blown her nose, Lucille said that it was important to know why she was crying all the time. And was immediately sorry for saying the words.

What are your plans? Lucille asked.

I'm going to stay here.

Have you contacted your professors?

She shook her head.

He's very persuasive, Lucille said.

He's strong. He knows what he wants.

And what you want? He knows that too?

Don't try to trick me, Mom.

I'm sorry. It's just that I worry. I wonder where he comes from, what other lives he's lived. If he has children.

He does. From an earlier relationship.

Libby said this blithely, almost too quickly, as if she wasn't aware of what it meant. Or as if she might be afraid of discovering exactly what it meant.

Oh, Libby. So he's a father.

Yes.

And he sees his children?

They come visit. I want you to like him. It's important. Come to the meeting tonight and listen to him. He's brilliant.

I don't think so. I've never understood what people mean when they say someone is brilliant.

It would just be easier for everyone if you wouldn't be so harsh. So cruel. It's the way you set your mouth. I can see the judgment.

Lucille was quiet. She herself could feel her judgment, a slick and slippery poison inside her. She said, If your father were here, Libby, he'd kidnap you. Take you home.

Libby made a face, something near disgust, and said that he'd already kidnapped a girl called Jill.

Are you doing this to get back at your father?

Your problem, Mom, is that you think this is about you. And Dad. Or Martin. None of that is true. I feel completely free here. Though Shane believes everything is about the father. A girl's woes.

Woes?

The father fucks you up.

His words?

Oh no. Shane would never swear. He's very clean. Very proper.

There's the outside, and then there's the inside. Is he clean inside?

Absolutely.

Do you want to make this bed? Lucille asked.

I do. I like my bed.

Why cry about it, then?

Maybe I'm crying because I'm happy.

Is he forcing you to have sex?

Mom. That's my business. And no, he's not. If anything, he's old-fashioned. Shane says we will wait.

Maybe it would be better if you tried it out. See if you like it with him.

You sound desperate, Mom. Is that why you came here? To convince me to have sex? God, that's perverted.

I wanted to meet this man. I wanted to see what group you'd fallen for. I see nothing rigorous, just young girls playing at house and being submissive. What *is* the point? Is he recruiting you for something?

That would make you happy, wouldn't it? Something concrete to point at and say, There, there is the problem. I will save Libby from *that*. There is nothing to save me from, Mom. Take a look at yourself instead, and your group.

My group?

Your age group. You've taken and taken until there is nothing left. And then Dad goes and takes some more by starting all over. As if he might live forever. Maybe he wants to live forever. All this taking. And what's left? No jobs, no water, no trees, no life, no money, nothing. Your grandchildren will be left with sand and cockroaches. Well done. Even flying here, calling it a detour, throwing more shit into the air.

But there were empty seats, Lucille wanted to say, and the plane would have taken off regardless. Though she knew, in her heart, that Libby was right. She, and those of her age, had plundered the planet. Morris's brother Samuel, a religious fanatic who lived in Montana, believed that the world would end on July 23, 2043, when Samuel would be ninety. Perfect. Samuel didn't have children. He didn't have to worry about the future. He needn't be concerned, he would be flying up to heaven. What twisted thinking was that? And yet, try to argue with Samuel and he just smiled and said that all news, and especially news that had to do with the climate and pandemics, was alarmist. False. He'd been heavily influenced by conspiracists, and those who passively waited to go to heaven while actively gobbling up the Earth. Those who were hiding from themselves. But here was Libby, not pointing a finger elsewhere, but simply at Lucille. And Lucille could only say, You are right. Absolutely right. And then she said that she had met Essie.

Oh, I love Essie.

She told me that she was chosen by Shane as well. But rejected him. Is that true?

She's taking a lot of detours.

She sounds pretty smart.

She is. But she's a bit unstable. Shane says that she has lots to learn.

Lucille said that she was going to Phuket for a week. She wanted Libby to come along.

I can't. I'd lose my place.

What place is that?

My place beside Shane. She gave a rueful smile. I'm not stupid, Mom. I know that what Shane says is sometimes way out there. And I know that most of the girls who have joined the community are very gullible. They just coast along and smile. I don't go along with everything. But

67

I really like Shane. I wasn't happy back home. I was in a competition. For the most beautiful life. I was good at competing. But it didn't satisfy me. I don't care about any of that anymore. Even as I talk to you, I don't care what you think. You can have your tantrums, and you can have your opinions, and you can try to convert me to your side, but it doesn't mean anything. I know myself now. My past was all a performance. This life here is not a performance.

But you're all dressed up. You have a script. What is that if not a performance?

We all have uniforms, Mom. You put one on. Every day.

Will you come with me? Lucille asked. To Phuket?

I might. I'll think about it. But don't expect me to change.

What about that night when you texted me? All that about being fucked up and lost. Was that nothing?

That was huge. I meant everything I said. And you were great. So non-judgmental. And then you asked if I liked these people. And I said I wasn't sure. And so, I had to assess my feelings. And my position here. With these people. And I saw that liking or not liking them had nothing to do with them. It was about me. Did I like myself? And I didn't, in that moment. I remember what you used to say: Do you know what you are doing, and are you okay with it? I hated that. I thought it was such an easy way to slip away from being responsible. My mother the flake. But you were right. And the strange thing is that I am willing to accept the consequences. Something I was never capable of doing. I'm in the moment, Mom. I'm okay with it. That's a good thing. Isn't it?

∞

In the morning, lying in her bed, she heard through her open window the happy cries of children in the pool below. She was still deeply affected by the sounds of children playing, for it brought her back to the early years with her three children. Her happiest recollections were the summer evenings, shadows stretching, and the children returning from the wild outdoors dirty and tired, and the baths she drew, and the bedtimes, and the reading, three wet heads crowded around her shoulders, and Morris looking in on them, and sometimes joining them, and now they were five, and life could not be any better. It would go on and on to infinity. She had been naively in love with the idea of perfection. And in the later years, when the children were older, and almost gone, she would come home from work and sit with Morris and they would drink wine and nibble at olives and she would ask about his day and his answer would be brief and uneventful — this was before the chaos of soul and mind — and then he would ask about her day and she would tell him about various patients, and he liked to hear the stories, and she liked to tell them, and she wondered, even then, if they weren't living vicariously through strangers' lives, or if they might have been experiencing a form of *schadenfreude*, happy to be exempt from the suffering of common and unfortunate citizens. This was all before, of course, when they were gloating in their good fortune. What calamity can appear without warning. They weren't prepared.

When they were still together, Morris loved to buy Lucille clothes. And she loved to receive them. Until she no longer did. And yet he persisted, and she began to see that he might have been looking for a younger and better Lucille. Buying clothes for her was a way of reinserting himself. He dressed her up! He bought her a short skirt once and asked that she wear it out to dinner with her black boots, and though she balked initially, she finally gave in, and she was pleased to give in, for she was suddenly relieved of the fight, of claiming her space, and if her acquiescence led to sex later, she was happy for that as well. Until she realized that she didn't have to have sex unless she wanted to, and she could choose her own clothes — though she often wondered why she was choosing a form-fitting dress or a cropped top — and her new autonomy confused Morris, for the patterns had now changed, and he became angry and called her stingy and stubborn, which led to a fight, and she would go silent and think that the marriage had to be over, but she also knew that his anger was his anger, and that her desire was her desire. Which was complicated for him, and simple for her. Or was it the other way around? And why such relief after sex? Because she feared his anger? And why had she enjoyed the sex so? Did it have to be so twisted?

It was about desire. Or projection of desire. Or the wish to fulfill desire. Or maybe projecting onto others what you wish to have projected back onto you. The flutter of it. The weird attack of desperate lust at the strangest times. Take Juan, the man who had been her professor in medical school and was still, years later, her supervisor and advised her on her cases. As a young student, she had recognized that Juan was a man she could admire in a deep and natural way. Those had been the years when she had acted with complete assurance and ignorance, as all medical students do, and Juan had corrected her, and in a not-so-gentle manner he had pointed out her faults and mistakes. One time — this was in her second year of medicine, when they met weekly for one-to-one sessions — she had shown up early and was crouched behind a chair, studying herself in her compact mirror, arranging her hair. He entered the room and found her in that manner. He asked what she was doing. She had been embarrassed, for he had caught her not only putting on makeup but hiding while she did so. She said that she was preparing for the supervision. He sat, and crossed his short legs, and he said that he didn't have sex with his students. Lucille had been speechless. What presumption. What audacity. And yet, when she went home that night and told Morris about the incident, she related the story in a heroic manner, and she sang Juan's praises. Look at what a safe man he was, gently saying no to sex.

Morris said that it was all very patriarchal. In fact, Juan certainly wanted to have sex with Lucille. That's why he had used those exact words. It wasn't about her actions; it was about his. Morris said that if he were Juan, he'd be lusting after Lucille as well. She was young and beautiful. Juan was old. Just the fact that he said those words, I don't have sex with my students, put him in a position of power and control. He probably got off on it.

Lucille shook her head and said that in Morris's world, everyone lost.

Do you want to fuck him? Morris asked.

Of course not. You're too literal, Morris.

But you were seducing him.

That was the strangest thing. I was applying lipstick. Plumping my hair. I wore your favourite skirt, the green plaid. My high red boots. I was outside of myself. Over there. Watching. But not really aware of what I was doing. And he brought me crashing down. He was so clear about boundaries.

You're such a pleaser.

Am I? Lucille asked. And she paused, and considered for a moment, and then said that Morris might be right. And to correct that, she would stop pleasing him.

Morris had laughed, and kissed her, and she kissed him back, and they poured Calvados, and talked and talked, and the talking and the Calvados, such a sweet nectar, had led to more kissing, and they ended up on the rug, half naked, and at some point — she remembered this very clearly, even now — she had imagined that Morris was Juan and it had filled her with hope and lust and just general disarray. Quite lovely.

That had been so long ago. Why this impossible nostalgia? She hated nostalgia. As did Juan, which was one of their affinities.

Juan was still her supervisor. She also saw Dr. Helguson, but that was for her own self, not for her work. Juan was much older now, and though he was overweight and occasionally rude and somewhat shrunken, she continued to love his mind, and the quickness there, and the words, and how to hear the words, and how to find the words, and how to say them.

Why the dresses? Lucille asked.

She was sitting in Shane's office. There was a gecko on the wall behind him. A fan turned slowly overhead. Shane behind a wooden desk. Lucille on the edge of a metal chair. She was wearing a light cotton printed dress that exposed her shoulders, and she wore sandals with numerous laces that came up to mid-calf. Greek-like. Which was interesting because she felt she had been asked to participate in a Socratic symposium, with Shane sitting in as the wise man. A session with Shane. These were the words he had used, and she had scoffed at them. Not outwardly. That would have been too arrogant, too dangerous. He appeared to be physically smaller on this day, more ascetic, a bit weak in the chin. And Lucille realized that he had shaved. Perhaps for this meeting? She could not know, but still, it was odd, for his beard had been substantial and now it was gone. And so, she now had a weak white chin to study. But still, he was good-looking. This was disturbing.

He smiled when she asked the question about the dresses. He said that most people liked order and uniformity. Especially those who were slightly lost.

And dressing up helps them find themselves?

Get rid of vanity, and competition, and even mirrors, and you will have time to look inside yourself, he said.

She asked him where the boys were. The men. Why were there only girls in the group?

He said that girls were more curious. And open. Softer. There had been boys who had joined them for a time, but they usually left. Most had authority issues.

Do you have sex with these girls?

You're very direct, Dr. Black. Why must everything be about sex?

Because it is always present. Even you not having sex with my daughter is about sex.

Libby told you that?

Daughters talk to their mothers, Lucille said. My daughter does.

That's wonderful, Shane said. You are lucky.

The thing is, Lucille said, I don't understand what this is all about. When she said the word *this*, she moved her hands outwards to take in the room and then brought her hands back to her lap. Do you want to save these girls? Do you want to save others? Yourself? Are you hiding from something? Would you even know?

I know myself, Shane said. And I know what others might think of me. You, for example, see me as a huckster, a smooth talker who has seduced your daughter with words. You are not the first to throw that at me. What responsibility does your daughter have in this? Where is she? Do you give her credit for thinking? For deciding, for wanting, for favouring?

She is not herself. She is lost. And I think you depend on her being lost. It's perverse really, very dangerous, and what's most dangerous is that neither you nor the girls see the danger. Or if you do, it sustains something. You get a dogged pleasure from locking up these girls. And I won't stand by and watch my daughter succumb to your poison.

She bowed her head. She had lost control. Her hands were shaking.

Shane poured a glass of water and slid it across the desk towards her. She took it and drank.

He smiled and said, Did you ever think that Libby might be telling you what she expects you want to hear? To placate you? To please you? You are enmeshed. The difference between men and women is that men are performers and women are victims. Men are angry. Women have to access their anger. This is why we have women here. They are allowed to access their anger. And it is usually directed at their parents.

She fascinates me, he said. As do you. I can see where she gets her fire. I told Libby that we are abandoned by our mothers from a young age. When the child realizes that the mother is with others. That is when the child understands that she is not the sole object of the mother's affection. That is when rejection begins. She gave me her father's memoir to read. I skimmed it. What ego. What lack of knowledge. Using your dead son, and your living daughters, as a launching pad to discuss his own issues. A father doesn't do that. A father leaves space for the child. And you, how much space have you left for your daughter? Why are you here? Why are you in this room? Where is Libby? Are you her spokesperson? No wonder she is confused.

She said, You are a father.

I am.

And your children?

They are living with their mother. In Australia.

So you are leaving space for your children.

He touched his left wrist with his fingertips. Did not say anything for a moment. Then sighed.

People wonder why I would abandon my children, he said. I've asked myself the same. And I have no good answer. Other than a sense of calling. A restlessness. I am selfish. That is certain. But I am okay with that. I am a better self for it. Ask Libby. We've discussed this over and over, the difference between self-interest and self-regard, or if corruption of the soul comes from the outside or the inside. She has interesting things to say. She has your acuity. Your intelligence.

You don't know me, Lucille said. Don't presume to.

You and I are equals, Dr. Black. We are not much different. Both of us are trying to help others.

That's fucking bullshit, she said. Don't you dare compare us.

There, Shane said, pointing a finger at her. There. I love it. The anger.

Lucille said that she would be taking Libby on a trip.

And Libby wants this?

She is coming. Willingly.

Well, then, she should go. Be with her mother.

You won't try to dissuade her?

This is not a prison. Everyone is free to come and go.

And I will try to convince her to not return here.

Of course. Once again, you will impose your will.

No. We will talk. And hopefully, she will come to her senses. Find herself.

Her voice was softer now, almost resigned. She was tired.

And which self will she be looking for? he said. Your version? My version? Her version? Someone else's version? Happy hunting.

Lucille stood and her chair tipped backwards. She looked down and saw that the lace from one of her sandals had come loose. She couldn't bend to fix it, because then she would have to bow before this man, and then he would see the back of her shoulders, and the back of her neck, and he would see what an old woman looks like when she is stooped and sorting her feet out. She could not do that. She had to now go. She adjusted her glasses, pulled at her skirt. She said, I am not a fool. Neither is my daughter. And she turned and walked out of the room, her lace trailing from her Greek sandal.

When Morris first announced that he was writing a memoir, Lucille thought, Oh my, what good can come of this? And then she thought that he would be one of those old men dredging memories, explaining away mistakes, making up a better version of himself, and he would finish it, and put it away in a box under his bed where he hid all of his important things, and that would be it.

And then, to his delight, and to her distress, his memoir was published and lauded as trenchantly honest and brutally intimate. Interviews. Profiles. Lucille had received a call from a journalist who was writing a piece on Morris Schutt. She said, No comment, and hung up. She was sure her cold response would be duly registered. And the readers of the profile, and the readers of Morris's book, would think what a lucky fellow Morris was to have escaped that harridan.

She had read his book in one sitting. For four months, she resisted picking it up. She was afraid. For herself, for the girls, for Morris, and, especially and most acutely, for Martin, who no longer had a voice, or any means to say, Dad, this is great. Or, Dad, this is all wrong. Of course, nothing was ever all wrong. But, sometimes, it could be mostly wrong. And in the case of the memoir, though Morris gave the appearance of honesty and soul-searching, he was still pointing away from himself, which was the ultimate irony.

If Lucille felt betrayed, how much more so would their daughters feel the disloyalty of his words? Of course, there were times when the writing soared — he captured so intimately that moment when they learned of Martin's death, and he showed himself struggling with his ego, and he revealed a few demons. This is to say that when he was writing about himself, he did an adequate job — though one can protest one's own culpability too much, and so what comes of those protests is a movement towards victimhood and woe-is-me, and what starts out as a shouldering of responsibility turns into a *volte-face*, and you end up with ambivalence and deflection.

If he wanted to pin himself like a captured insect on the cardboard of his own existence, and then mount that cardboard for all to see, so be it. But to take Meredith, and to take Libby, and to lay out their lives, and to mention the names of their lovers and boyfriends, and to speak of their grief as if it were his, that was just vulgar. And wrong. He had been too noisy in his tone. Pornographic with his sorrow. He had heaved himself onto the pommel horse of his ego and flexed his intellectual muscle, only the muscle was weak. He had hidden behind the great thinkers. Played hide-and-seek with his emotions. Not faced himself. He should have burned the manuscript.

This was the age of yelling. And Morris, in his piece of writing, had become just one more yeller. Why? To what end? So that he could become famous for a few more minutes? Did he miss his column and all those adoring writers of letters who had fawned over him? People loved *true* stories. Readers adored the personal. They wanted the underbelly. They wanted ugliness. And then they wanted redemption.

A memoir had the possibility of being complex, for it held a narrative, but within the narrative and the ultimate renewal, the writer often tumbled into a surprising lack of rigour. The precision of the self was usurped by exclamation marks. The emotion! The hyperbole! The restoration! Here indeed was a sphincter problem. Morris had held on to his shit (sort of) for a long time and then, in one glorious squat, sprayed it everywhere. She had been astounded to read about a particular blow job that she had given him years ago in a moment of passion and release. Not only had he put words in her mouth, he'd gone ahead and put his cock in her mouth. She hadn't blown him, ever, after Martin died. It was before. When they were still a couple. When they were still in love. When they made love. It had happened many times. Why just mention that one time? She had come off as prudish and parsimonious. And the marriage had come off as calamitous. She had controlled him. She had been tight-fisted in love. She had made him build the deck and renovate the kitchen. None of this was true. That had been Morris looking for something to occupy himself. He'd had great gaps of free time. He spent thirty minutes every morning spilling into his column, and then he puttered around the house the rest of the day. And, to be fair, she had been the beneficiary of that freedom. He made great salads. Asian salmon. Thai food. He cleaned the floors. He sat down to pee. He had been her lover and her maid, and perhaps he resented that. Perhaps he felt emasculated, which was an unfortunate word, for it assumed that one was potent to begin with. What was the female equivalent of that particular word? Defeminize? Unsex? Whatever it was, it didn't carry the same gravity, the same consequence, which was a reflection of the limits of language. The one thing Morris got right in his memoir was that Lucille made more money than him. And always had. Yet he presented this as a sin. A fault. What was wrong with making money? Who would pay the bills? We can't all be artists, drinking espresso in our garret and looking longingly out the dirty window at the clouds flitting by. Doing nothing. Producing nothing. Yet waiting, waiting, for that brilliant inspiration that will shoot us to glory.

She had known, of course, that he would want to know what she thought. He still needed her approval. In fact, right after it was published, he asked her if she'd read the memoir yet. She said no. She wasn't sure if she'd ever read it. Then she said, Give me some time.

How much time?

I don't know, Morris. Five years?

You're still bitter, Lucille.

Am I? I don't think bitter is the right word. Afraid, perhaps. Or just tired.

There's nothing to be afraid of. I did you no harm. In fact, I was generous towards you.

I'll let you know, she said. And she hung up.

In June, after Lucille had read the memoir, Meredith visited and saw the book lying on the coffee table. She picked it up and asked, You read it?

I did.

And?

I'm not sure. I'm too close.

Did he talk about me?

Some.

Did he talk about Jill?

Just at the end, as a sort of new-path kind of thing. A future. Hope.

Bullshit, Meredith said. He's living in a fucking nursery rhyme. And I know, I know because I've seen this kind of thing before. Dad will fall down, and Jill will leave him. She's too smart. She's my age, good God. It's vile. And of course, now they have the baby and he has a new family. I asked him the other day about his old family. Us. What about us? Libby and me? He got all sheepish and maudlin and said he loved us forever. Jesus.

Lucille felt a great pang. Unlike Morris, she could not renew herself, she could not have a baby, she could not sidestep, even briefly, the inevitable march towards death. She felt she should cry out, say something, but she didn't want to feed Meredith's outrage, and so she kept quiet.

He's like a teenager, Mom. It's embarrassing. Does it make you sad? The baby?

Not sad. I don't want any more children. I'm happy for them.

Really?

Okay, maybe I'm indifferent.

He whistles a lot these days.

Meredith was too occupied, too consumed, by the lives of others, in particular Morris's life. Lucille told her that. She said that Meredith needed to get away from her father. It wasn't healthy to still be living with Morris. And Jill. A new family needed space. You need space, she said. It's not healthy for Jake.

Jake's fine. He's very malleable. And easygoing. He likes Jill. What's not to like? She's beautiful, and full, and young, and fun. Makes me feel old.

You're not old.

I feel old. And I have found a new place, an apartment close to Bar Italia. I can just walk to work.

The day following the conversation with Meredith, Morris phoned and left a message. He spoke her name softly, almost apologetically, and then said, Could we talk?

He called back two days later, and this time she answered.

You're there, he said.

Yes.

How are you?

What is it, Morris?

I left you a message.

Yes, you did.

You didn't call.

To say what?

To talk about the memoir. Meredith told me you'd read it.

And you couldn't wait? Give me some time?

I thought you might be angry.

Do you want to ask a question?

Are you angry?

Why would you think that?

Because I fucked up. Because I included you in my memoir. And our children. Which might have been wrong, but impossible to avoid, given that it was a memoir. Are you there?

I am.

What did you think?

You're a good writer, Morris.

Thank you. Just good? Not great?

That would be for others to state. Not me. I'm not a critic.

True. But I trust you. I saw every crack, every flaw, every misstep, and no matter how much I edited myself, new cracks and flaws popped up.

The duck-hunting scene was tender. I saw Martin then.

Wasn't it? That just rolled off the pen. So real. He was there.

I'm glad, Morris.

Thank you, Lucille. You're being very generous. You are, and I appreciate it. Are you being honest?

What do you want?

What I've always wanted. Your love. Your admiration. I want you to say that I'm brilliant. I want you to tell me one thing that was wrong in the memoir.

Don't do this, Morris.

What? I'm absolutely serious. I need to know where I've failed.

Your false modesty has not gone away.

Is that right? You see. This is what I need. A clear response. I remember, years ago, back when you still analyzed me in the kitchen, in the bedroom, on the tennis court, and you said that I was weary of people, and that this weariness was a neurotic arrogance, and you said that I always had to be first but was afraid to be first. Which is why I always let you win in tennis.

I beat you, Morris, you didn't let me win. In any case, this is too much. I have to go.

You probably didn't like the sex in the book.

I didn't. The blow job was especially gratuitous.

Really? Gratuitous? How? It was one line in a three-hundred-page book. It was the interpretation of that act that was crucial. I believe I mentioned tenderness, and I spoke of sex and death, and my regrets, and I spoke of my lust, and the sadness I experienced as I held your head like a golden bowl, and the tears you shed later, and the disgust you had for yourself. And for me. For being alive when Martin was dead. Why focus on the act, when it was the act that led to the saddest of epiphanies? Speaking of golden bowls. When my mother was dying at Donwood, and my father was still robust and cognizant, we sat at her bedside, listening to her drag in ponderous breaths, and my father and I spoke of Ecclesiastes 12, and he asked me to read it, and so I did. The King James Version. I recall the third verse vividly: *In the day when the keepers of the house shall tremble, and the strong men shall bow themselves, and the grinders cease because they are few, and those that look out of the windows be darkened*. And my father halted me, and he said that the keepers were the hands, and the strong men were the legs, and the grinders were the teeth, the windows were the eyes. I was amazed, for though I had been forced to memorize this passage as a boy, I had never understood the meaning, but now, as my mother was dying, I marvelled at the poignancy there. Oh, this is what we yearn for—that our children might reach the age of bowing and trembling and ceasing and darkening.

Are you reading this, Morris? Did you write this out in advance? I won't be waylaid in this manner.

No. No. Let me finish. I have failed. And though I am faithless, I do believe that we will be brought into judgment, every secret thing, whether it be good, or whether it be evil. This book, this piece of drivel as you would call it, is my secret thing.

Not so secret anymore, is it? And I don't think it's drivel. You are incapable of writing drivel.

That's a lovely sentiment.

Please. Morris.

It's been over a year since we've talked. Actually talked liked this.

This is you talking.

You know, of course, that I am a father again. Jill and I had a little boy.

Yes. I heard.

He's very sweet. Beautiful. Henry Martin.

Oh. Oh.

Have you heard from Libby?

Some.

She sounds very happy. That's good. I was quite worried about her.

Goodbye, Morris.

She had not known about the namesake. It broke her heart. And that Jill, who had never known Martin, should participate in the stealing of the name. This was devastating. In her darkest moments, she found herself wishing that the child would die, so that Jill could experience the desolation of loss. And then she woke, and she was terrified by her thoughts and her wishes. Her vindictive nature had all been sorted through long ago, and she had believed that the frantic search for understanding herself was in the past. And now, here she was, once again, a tiny animal lost in the forest, shuttling back and forth between this trail and that trail, and not knowing where this or that trail led.

She too wanted a baby named Martin.

She told her mother this, and her mother, who sometimes could not recall her own children's names, had said, Of course you do, Lucille. Of course. And you should have one. And I wish it. My heart aches for you.

Oh, Mom.

Is the baby alive?

Yes, he is. He is a month old.

Can I see him?

He's not mine to show.

I know. I know. But to see him would be lovely.

Her mother called the following day and said that she had to see this little Henry before she died. It was essential. And on another note, strangers were in her home and they were in the process of making lunch, and then they would do dishes, and this was the last thing she needed.

Those are the home care workers, Mom, Lucille said. This isn't for you, it's for me. I don't have time to make all your meals, or clean your apartment, and this eases the burden.

What about my burden? her mother said. Really. It's an invasion of privacy. I've been working so hard. All my life. After your father went bankrupt, I went to work. And then he died. And I kept working. And now, here I am, and it is the end, and I pace my apartment, muttering, What shall I do? What shall I do?

I understand, Mother. It's hard.

You don't understand. You have a career. You have your three children. You are vibrant. There will come a day, Lucille, when you will be wearing my shoes, pacing your own little place and wondering how you got there. It is unavoidable.

Would you like to go out for lunch? Lucille asked. I can pick you up.

Her mother hesitated. And finally said yes. That would be good.

Her mother was wearing a summer dress, printed pink and white, and white running shoes, and she carried her purse, and she wore sunglasses. She climbed into Lucille's Audi and said, You got a new car.

It's not, Mom.

It smells new. And it feels new. Your father used to give me a new car every year. Right up until he lost everything.

How does that happen? I took everything for granted. Money, cars, food, travel, clothes. Don't ever do that.

Never, Lucille said. And this was the truth. After her father's personal bankruptcy, she watched him descend into anarchy. He bought lottery tickets, hoping to reclaim by some fluke everything he had lost. He invested what little he had left in schemes that gave him no return. *Reader's Digest* Sweepstakes was one. Publishers Clearing House was another. And it was the latter scheme that flooded his mailbox with little trinkets — shot glasses, vases, toy cars, tiny spoons — all neatly stored in the hall closet and never used. And then her father took sick and died quite quickly. As if he had willed it. And here was her mother, years later, insisting on living, pressing onwards, too fearful to die, too despondent to enjoy the life of the undead.

And now, in the cocoon of the car, Lucille asked her mother where she would like to eat. Applebee's, her mother said. Lucille suggested that a change might be nice, and her mother did not argue. And so, they went to Café Carlo and sat at a table for two and her mother ordered seafood pasta. Lucille had salad. Her mother said that yesterday she had driven out to the village and spent the night with Elmira. Lucille asked the name of the village. Where was it? Her mother could not recall. But it was nearby, not a long drive.

Lucille said, You know that Elmira died five years ago.

Did she? Oh, my. I don't know anymore. I must have gone to her funeral. Did I?

You did. I was with you.

Well, her mother said. I did go to the village. It was quite pleasant. Like the old days. I slept in the same bed with a woman who I thought was Elmira. But if she is dead, as you say, and I'm not sure you're right, then it must have been another friend.

You used to drive out to Steinbach and visit Rosanne. You and she would share a bed.

Yes, of course. It was Rosanne. Funny thing. How's Morris?

I haven't been with Morris for a long time, Mom.

Really? I'm so sorry.

In her early twenties, when Lucille had just started university, her mother would meet Lucille downtown at the Grill Room. And her mother, happier finally and more level, would talk and talk about her friends, about fights with Lucille's father, about her sex life, and about her orgasms. Lucille listened, was thrilled to have a mother as a best friend—it made up for all those lost years when her mother had been ill—and at no point did she think that this was too intimate, or that her mother's sex life was none of her business. After lunch, the two of them would go shopping for lingerie, and her mother asked about men in Lucille's life, and here too, Lucille told her everything. And then Morris came into Lucille's life, and her mother fell in love with him. And was afraid of him. Didn't want to be in the same room alone with him. He was far too good-looking. Her mother had been extremely upset when Lucille had left Morris. Why would she do that? He was a man who did everything for her. He cooked, he cleaned, he was gentle, he was kind, he was magnanimous. Lucille just had to try harder. She was too inflexible. Even as a child, she was judgmental of others, of her friends. Her standards were far too high. This could only lead to grief and discord and sadness. There was enough sadness in the world. You have to take care of the man in your life, Lucille, her mother had announced. Men are highly sensitive, they can be hurt easily, are not very smart emotionally, and if you don't pay attention to their needs, they will run away.

All of this advice was something her mother might have heeded herself.

But these were wayward memories. Pay attention to the present. Right now, her mother was sitting across from her, pursuing a piece of shrimp around the plate, and when she finally captured it, she lifted it with a shaking fork to her mouth. The shrimp escaped and tumbled down the cloth of her dress and left a trail of olive oil. She tried again, with another piece of shrimp, and this time succeeded.

The conversation, what there was of it, broke up into bits and pieces. First Libby. And then one small mention of Martin. Another brief foray into Morris, who was a fine man. And then Jake, who was on a flag football team. And then a reminiscence about a cruise she had taken with her husband, Gerald. The grandeur. And a dinner in Vienna. With an orchestra playing. And then a conversation about her eight-year absence. She had been sick. Her memory was erased.

One Saturday, visiting her mother, she found her lying on the couch. Her teeth were on the coffee table. She was relaxing. Lucille tidied while her mother talked. She said that Lucille was always too busy. She should sit down. Lucille agreed but kept working. She did the dishes. She cleaned the bathroom. Made the bed. They called out to each other as Lucille worked. Her mother had very good hearing. At one point, Lucille came back into the living room, where her mother was listening to Gram Parsons. She was swooning. The song ended. She looked at Lucille and made the world with two arms. Stretched upwards. The skin on her arms was very slack, and it hung loose. Her mother said, If you take it all, all of it, and squeeze out what's bad — and here she made two fists and squeezed until she was trembling — you squeeze and squeeze, she said. Here she laid her hands down on her lap. Opened them. You're left with something wonderful, she said. And then she looked down at her open hands.

Lucille picked up Libby from the compound at four in the morning and they walked to the bus station through streets that were still alive with hawkers and tourists and the possibility of sex. They took a bus up to Bangkok and then a taxi to the airport, and from there they flew down to Phuket, where they found a hotel for the night, with plans to take a boat over to the island of Phi Phi the following day. In Phuket, Libby was still wearing her dress. She came out of the bathroom, freshly showered, her hair out of the braid, the shoulders of her jean dress damp. She kept checking herself in the full-length mirror in the foyer of the room. She had not spoken much during the bus ride. And during the flight, sitting by the window, she pressed her forehead against the pane, and then slept, for her hand jumped once, and she gave a little cry, and then she did not move.

Lucille read. She had brought along a novel by a female writer whom Morris had recommended. Morris, to her surprise and perhaps his, still sent her notes about books. Read this one. Try this. He had said that this particular author had a voice that Lucille might find interesting and compelling. She did. There was very little dialogue, everything was said indirectly, and the narrator was elusive. She was a listener, and she managed to get the people around her to reveal themselves in intimate ways. Every character who spoke in the indirect voice sounded the same, analytical and almost self-aware, but not quite. Nothing really happened in the novel, much was interior, and yet the story accrued power and beauty in the manner that coral will slowly build itself over time and then become an organism to look at, and yet dangerous to get too close to.

Libby had a tattered and much-read copy of *The Bell Jar*. She had read it first at sixteen, and then many times since, and was now carrying it around with her, holding it in her lap, not opening it, just letting it rest, even as she slept. Lucille worried that there was something pathological in this attachment to a story that did not end well.

They ate a late lunch of hamburgers and fries on the terrace of the restaurant that was attached to the hotel. Libby ate ferociously, her eyes and mouth wide open. She was sloppy, and spilled mayonnaise on her dress. She wiped at it with a napkin. She ordered dessert, ice cream with caramel sauce. This too she attacked.

She sat back finally and patted her stomach. She said that Morris had sent her a photo of Jill pregnant, just before the baby was born. As if she too might want to celebrate with them. She said that she'd been upset with the name choice. She had wanted to call *her* baby Martin. When she had one. She said that she couldn't remember her brother anymore. Not really. He was gone. She said she sometimes thought that, when she died, the saddest thing would be the forgetting. People forget, she said. And they move on. And they don't think about you anymore. And you disappear.

Lucille said that Martin wasn't forgotten.

How often do you think of him?

Every day.

But at some point, when we die, Martin will disappear. There will be no one else to remember. It happens to everyone. Unless you're Cleopatra, or Shakespeare. And then the remembering is faulty, and myths are created. Who were they, truly?

She said that she had told Shane about Martin. About his death. And she'd been immediately sorry. She said, People listen to your story and then they connect it to their own story, and so now it is their story that becomes important, and the original story gets lost. No one wants to really know about my life, or your life, or someone else's life.

Lucille said that she didn't agree. The reason she loved her job was the complexity of the story. People tell me things, and as I listen to them, I see how intricate relationships are, and how difficult it is to peel back the layers and the arguments and the protection.

But you *have* to listen to them. They pay you. And you're not allowed to talk about yourself. Which is not the real world.

It's real. As real as us here right now. Or you listening to Shane talk. Or that couple over there. The old man with the Thai girl.

Yeah. I saw them earlier. I can tell you exactly where that girl comes from. I know these girls from teaching them English. She comes from the north and was sold by her family at the age of fourteen. The family got enough money to buy a pickup. She ended up in Patpong or Pattaya, and she's had every kind of sex possible, dangerous sex, and she is hoping to meet a foreign man who will marry her and take her back to his country. It never happens. Or maybe it happens once or twice, and this is why the girls are hopeful. She might get lucky.

They were quiet. Then Libby said, What is this wedding you're going to? Who is it?

Baptiste.

A man?

Yes.

How old is he?

Your age. Just a friend.

Really? That's weird. How do you know him?

We met at Sally's son's wedding. He was an exchange student.

So you knew him well. If he's invited you to his wedding.

Well enough.

Why so secretive?

No secrets. He was new to the city. We met. We liked the same things.

You hung out?

It was nothing.

Mom. I didn't say it was. Why so defensive?

I'm not. He was sweet and lonely and we became friends.

Just friends?

Yes. I cooked for him. He was too skinny. Ate poorly. I liked speaking French with him. He practised his English.

Libby laughed.

What?

You're so transparent.

Oh, Libby. You are imagining a certain kind of story. Anyway, he's getting married. And good for him, Lucille said.

And so, Libby abandoned the subject. Satisfied perhaps. Or more interested in herself. And Lucille was happy to not speak of Baptiste. There was not much to say. Or there was too much to say, and it was none of Libby's concern.

She had met Baptiste at the wedding of her friend Sally's son, a wedding she was late for because she couldn't find anything to wear. In the end, she had chosen a grey dress of light cashmere that held her body in a flattering manner. Not too revealing around her belly. A high neckline. A hem that fell to just below her knees, and could be rolled up for dancing, should she decide to dance. A small Coach bag to hang on to — Meredith had found it for her at a second-hand store. Chie Mihara pumps, black with white spots, easy on her arches.

At the reception, which was held beneath a large tent on the grounds of a lush park, she found herself beside Baptiste, who was spending a year in Canada. He had come to Winnipeg to finish out his final year in architecture. It was for his English, he said, and it was to study under a specific professor who was at the university for a year, on loan from a university in Budapest. This was why he had come here. Without being prompted, he gave an assessment of the city. It was small. The roads were awful for cycling, which was what he liked to do. The city sprawled in the manner that all urban settings do. The downtown was eclectic. There were some very ugly buildings. And some beautiful ones. Especially the old warehouses down by the river. They would make good office spaces, or apartments. Low-income housing. He was not impressed by the culture of the city. Everything was about hockey. Which he found amusing, until one of his professors took him to a game. And he fell for the sport. He said that hockey suited the city. It was violent and rough and yet there was a beauty there, and if you looked close enough, you could find it. Not easy to see at first, but then suddenly it appeared. You discover that it is not sophisticated, he said. And you are arrogant and disdain it for a time. And then, the longer you stay with it, you begin to realize that the lack of sophistication has its own beauty. It was not subtle. It was in your face. He said that he was aware of the poor of the city, and one day he had gone to the mall on Portage Avenue and he was shocked. There were no white people at the mall, save for the security guards, or the office workers on the second floor. But in the food court, it was wildly black and brown. So many people with so much time on their hands. Huddling away from the cold. And happy. Visiting. He wondered if the original builders of the mall had envisioned this.

He asked her what she did.

I am a psychiatrist.

You have your own practice?

I do.

Perhaps I should come see you, he said. Though it would be hard. My English is not great.

Lucille said that she had studied with a woman from Hong Kong, whose first language was Cantonese, and though this woman was working in English, she was always the first to understand a concept, and she was brilliant at insight. The psyche does not require translation, she said.

Disorder is a universal language. In any case, your English is very good. And you do not appear to need help with your psyche.

He smiled and said that he was very capable at hiding what was difficult inside him.

She smiled and said, That can be a good thing at a public event like this.

There were others at the table, some in conversation, some eating and drinking, others looking for conversation perhaps. Lucille said, You must have other people to talk to here.

Baptiste looked surprised, and said, But I am here. Beside you.

He asked if she was married.

She said that she was still married on paper but had been separated from her husband for a long time. And so, they were certainly no longer married. She said that it was amazing how many young people were getting married these days. It was so hopeful. The fact was that marriage was ultimately disappointing and most were bound to fail, and even if the couple stayed together, there was often a deleterious force of habit that shaped a long relationship, and one either lived with it or ran from it. She hoped that this marriage would be an exception. She said that she was sorry, she shouldn't have been so critical, so negative. It wasn't like her.

He asked her what the word *deleterious* meant. She told him.

He said, When you tell people what your job is, do they immediately begin to confide in you?

It happens. I don't like to tell people what I do.
But you told me.
I did.
So you want me to confide?
Do you want to?
I do. But not now. It would take too long.

She told her supervisor, Juan, that she was thinking of falling in love with someone half her age. This was several months after she had met Baptiste, and her mind had been whistling with thoughts, and in the mornings she felt a slight ache near the left side of her chest, and she found herself wanting to phone or text him, but she didn't. Juan asked Lucille why she had used the word *thinking*. And then he talked about the word *falling* and he wondered if it was possible to think while one was falling, to think in a clear and logical manner, or would one just panic, and perhaps try to flap one's arms futilely, and then he wondered if someone half Lucille's age would have half of her wisdom. And then he asked how she felt.

Wild, she said. And confused. And happy. Love is difficult to find. And keep. I'm getting older. He turns my head. And my heart. I see myself differently. She said that the other day, the young man she was speaking of had said that he loved her hands. The texture of her skin that showed off her fine bones. And later, she found herself looking at her hands and marvelling.

She didn't tell him that they weren't having sex. It was none of his business. Or maybe she wanted Juan to think that they were having sex. In any case, she danced around the topic, saying that she recalled something Juan had said long ago, about young people and sex. About when young people have sex, they are holding on to someone when they haven't learned to hold on to themselves. It was about a lack of skin, a lack of identity. Two anxious people hanging on to each other, and in order to give it meaning, they call it love. She said that she felt like a young person again. Perhaps she was lacking skin. Identity. There was certainly chaos in her life. And she knew that, in times of chaos, one's thinking became very black and white. But in the end, she said, it wasn't about the physical. It was his mind. She loved the elasticity there. Which certainly sounded predictable. She wondered out loud if it was illegal.

Juan smiled.

And then she said that it was certainly regressive.

He smiled again.

She said that she had become Morris, her ex-husband. This was something he would do. She said that after their son died, Morris fled into the arms of escorts. She said, Imagine what Morris would say now if he knew.

He might applaud, Juan said. And understand. And I don't think this man is the equivalent of an escort. Are you paying him?

Lucille laughed, almost out of obligation, for she didn't feel like laughing. She sometimes found Juan's sense of humour tiring and egotistical. Still, she laughed, and he was pleased.

She said that she worried about her daughters as well. That they would judge her.

They might not care.

Libby would care. She has a self-righteous streak. This boy is near to Libby's age. The strangest thing is, he seems to have no fear. But I do.

So, tell him you're afraid.

But I don't even know what I'm afraid of. I think I'm in love but haven't told him. Though I think he knows. And he doesn't speak of love, and I can't speak for him.

Then don't speak for him. Speak for yourself.

To say what?

Speak of love.

I keep wondering what he wants. And then thinking that it doesn't matter what he wants. All I know is that I don't want to be careful.

You can't know what he wants. He might not know. And even if he told you, it might not be true. And even if it wasn't true, you still have to address what you want. What do you want, Lucille?

Baptiste texted her during the day, and in the evenings. Innocent little notes. *Eating at Clementine*, and a photo of the eggs lying on a biscuit and a thick slice of bacon. *At the art gallery. They have one Monet!* Or, *Rented skates at the Forks. I am falling*, and a photo of him on skates, in the middle of the river trail, ankles bent, grinning. There was a girl beside him, holding him up. Lucille typically wrote back in the evening, and in that single text, she tried to cover everything he had sent her. *So fun*, she wrote. She felt like a teenager.

He came for a meal, every Friday. He kissed her on the cheek at the door, three times, making her dizzy, and he always told her that she was beautiful. He liked to touch her while she cooked, on the arm or the back. And each touch produced a shiver, and desire, which was not acted upon.

On one of these evenings, he told her that he had admired her immediately at the wedding. He said, You turned to me and talked about the poison of marriage.

I certainly didn't say poisonous, Lucille said.

Not that word exactly. But a word I didn't know. Similar to poison. And I thought, Whoaa. Strange. But at the same time, I thought, Oh, here is someone. He said that he hadn't seen the words as cynical or mean, but very straightforward, and not only had the words moved him to like her, but it was her mouth, and the manner of the slight twist upwards on the left side, that he had adored. Immediately. And of course, your dress. And your dancing. And your energy. And your eyes. And your bare feet.

On that evening, when he said these words, they were sitting across from each other at her small table in the nook at the back of her house. She had made salmon, and green beans, and a salad with a lemon zest dressing. She had changed her clothes three times before his arrival, and on her bed upstairs, the cast-off clothes lay in a scattered pile. In the end, she had chosen pants with a slight flare, and sandals, and a loose, ginger-coloured top that was sleeveless. A brave decision for her, because she did not like what gravity had done to her arms. But she wanted him to see her, and to accept her, or perhaps she wanted him to recognize that she was too old. Or he might see that she was in fact young enough. What craziness.

One time, she had asked him how old a woman would have to be in order for him to think that she was too old. And as soon as she said this, she was embarrassed. For she was fishing, and she didn't like how obvious her question was.

He smiled and said, Too old for what?

You know. Don't be coy.

Do you mean attraction?

Sure, why not? she said. Attraction.

He said that attraction was a very general term. Sometimes, how a woman talked, or how she moved through a room, with confidence, could be extremely attractive, even if she did not conform to the standards of beauty. The world's standards. Not his. He had spoken with young women who, from a distance, appeared stunning, and he imagined he'd like to know them in a specific way, or so he thought, and then one word dropped from their mouths and the lust disappeared. So, attraction was always surprising. Desire was surprising. This was why it would be better to be blind for a time when you first met someone. Words told you everything. And smell.

She herself had a keen sense of smell, and had known, even as a young woman, that certain men were more interesting to her because of their smell. Not in any obvious way, but in a deeply organic manner. And that is what happened with Baptiste: she smelled him and she was immediately taken with him.

She began to hone up on her French. She had studied it

in high school, and continued to take courses in university, and had lived in Montréal between her first and second years of school, where she had become nearly fluent, but after years of not speaking or reading, she was out of practice, and her vocabulary had fallen away. She bought a course on iTunes, a six-hour intensive taught by Michel Thomas, and because she had a foundation, and was merely brushing up on that foundation, she leaped ahead to level six and found herself working on lengthy sentences with negatives and numerous pronouns.

She listened to Michel at night, when she couldn't sleep. On the recording, he worked with two students, both apparently new to French, and both slower to answer than Lucille, and she found herself berating these students, for their ineptitude and their poor pronunciation. She asked Baptiste to speak French with her, and he did, but after half an hour, her mind was exhausted, and because his English was better than her French, they switched back to English.

She liked having him to herself. When he suggested going out to a restaurant, she said that she preferred to cook. She felt freer at home, no one was watching, and it was private. Though there was nothing to hide.

Sally sensed that something was going on. Had sensed it already at the wedding reception, when Lucille and Baptiste danced together, and he clung to her, quite drunk, and whispered that she was lovely, so lovely, and she did, at that time, recognize a split inside of him, and she allowed him to hold her. Sally, that night, whispered in her ear that Baptiste was attracted to Lucille.

I don't think so, Lucille said, and laughed dismissively.

Oh yes. I can see, Sally said. And she walked off to find her son, with whom she then danced.

For the rest of that evening, chagrined, Lucille avoided Baptiste, and when he finally found her again and sloppily kissed her on one cheek, and then another, and tried to drag her back onto the dance floor, she said that her legs were tired, and he should find a girl his age, there were many. And she moved her hand out towards the crowd on the dance floor. And he obeyed her. Later that night, just before she left the reception, she saw him holding a tiny girl, certainly not more than eighteen, and they were laughing and cavorting, and the little girl was looking up at this French man whose demeanour was soft and open and a little desperate.

The relationship with Baptiste was a cliché, but she understood that this was exactly the allure. When she was with her patients, she found herself thinking about sex. She sympathized more easily with the men who came to her and confessed that they were unhappy with their sex lives. And the women who had affairs. She silently cheered the women on. And asked the questions she asked all her patients: Do you know what you are doing, and are you okay with it?

She asked herself these same questions, and she said, Yes, I know, and I'm okay.

But that could have been trickery. And self-delusion. How do you truly know until the consequences tumble down around your neck? Her neck. Lately, she had studied herself in the mirror and wondered if she should get a slight tuck, ever so slight, so that her neck was tauter, and while the doctor was at it, maybe the chest area just below the neck, where the skin had become crepe-like and made her appear older than she actually was. But what did that mean? She was the age she was, and how could one appear older? She had lived many, many more years than Baptiste. She had children. He had none. She was wiser. She was sadder. Though he had certainly made her less wise, and less sad.

On the night when they ate fish and green beans and salad, as a single candle flickered on the table, and after he told her how he had fallen in love with her mouth and her dress and her dancing, she listened to him speak and she took his hand and asked if he had met someone yet.

He asked what she meant by "someone."

A girl. Or a boy, if you prefer.

I do, he said. During the six days when I do not see you, there are others. Both men and women.

Good. She said this quickly, and she smiled as she spoke, but inside, she was devastated.

Not true, he said.

Oh, you. Really?

He nodded. And then he said, Why would I find another? I have you.

But she knew that there had to be others. He was young. He was free. He was beautiful. She had told him once that it was possible to live many lives. Which was the opposite of what she told her patients. And so, now she was bending the truth and feeding herself lies. For wasn't it true that when she talked to him about the possibility of other lives, she was ultimately talking to herself?

One Friday night, in late October, several months into their relationship, he showed up with a crown of fresh snow on his long dark hair, and he entered the house and unwrapped himself from his tangled scarf and hung his coat and came in bearing flowers and wine and he gathered her up and hugged her and kissed her on the mouth. This was different from the usual three kisses on her cheeks, and she was surprised, but tried to not look surprised. And then they separated, and she said, Come.

She pulled him into the kitchen and continued cooking while he leaned on the counter and watched and plucked a warm cashew from a plate. She slapped his hand.

Taking a bath several hours earlier, she had sunk into the deep and hot water and rested there and been aware of her body beneath the surface, and at some point, she had begun to cry. She did not know where the tears had come from. When she was finished crying, she sat up and she shaved her armpits and her legs, lifting one leg at a time onto the edge of the tub. She had always been shy. A little timid with her body. Not trusting it. If her mind was her best friend, easy to understand and love and have a relationship with, her body was a stranger that she had always been wary of, as if it might deceive her, or turn against her. A ridiculous notion, for a body simply was. You could improve it with running or weights or cycling or swimming, and you might build up some muscle, and you could dress it up with clothes and makeup and a visit to a hair salon, but this body was yours and no one else's and so it only made sense to accept it. She could do that sometimes. When she had had a fair amount to drink, she became liberated. I love my legs, she had cried out the previous weekend, raising a calf for him to see. The music, the conversation, Baptiste grinning from across the room. From over there.

Open more wine, she told him now.

He obeyed. Poured them each a glass.

They drank. Looked at each other. Smiled.

They never talked about the week, or what the other had done. They never mentioned others. She did not talk about her patients, and he did not talk about school or friends. She knew very little about his past and his family and his background, and he knew less about hers. There were photos of her daughters in the house, and Martin in uniform, and of her grandson Jake, but he did not ask about them, which she found slightly disappointing. Perhaps he didn't care. Perhaps he was allowing her her privacy. He studied her bookshelf and sometimes pulled out a book and flipped through it. One time, he held up a book by Horney and asked if it was worthwhile. She said it was, especially for the long case study of a woman who had learned to analyze herself.

Why would you want to do that? he asked.

Why wouldn't you? she said.

They ate, they talked about what they were eating, they discussed the texture of different foods, they drank various wines and shared opinions on the wine, and in this area he had lots to teach her, for he was a bit of an oenophile. He did not say where he had learned this. She did not ask. When they were finished eating, they left the dirty dishes on the table and they went to sit by the fire. They might watch a film together on her laptop, their arms and hips touching, and if he was tired, he fell asleep, his head on her shoulder, while she finished the show. They were in the midst of *The Sopranos*, a show he had never seen. She'd watched it. Not for the thrill of the violence, but often to observe Melfi, the psychiatrist. Lucille loved Melfi. She wanted to be Melfi. She pointed out to Baptiste how Melfi sat. The clothes she wore. The cars she drove. How collected she was. And when Tony edged into sexual territory, she did not get hooked. Look at how she handles this, Lucille said to Baptiste.

You aren't allowed to have sex with your patients? Baptiste asked.

No.

After?

After when?

After they are finished, and time has passed.

That's okay. But it wouldn't work.

Have you fallen in love with a client?

No, I haven't.

But it is possible.

She didn't answer.

On this particular night, the evening when he had kissed her on the mouth, they moved from the kitchen to the living room. He sat on the couch as usual, but this time, she sat on the chair across from him.

Did I frighten you earlier? he asked.

It was not the usual greeting.

I was happy to see you.

And me you.

Yes?

Of course, she said. I look forward to these evenings. It's just that you can't go kissing a woman without asking.

It's very awkward to ask. Out the window goes freedom.

She said that there was a certain kind of man who existed in the world, and that type of man believed that he was free to kiss whomever, whenever. It had little to do with attraction or intimacy. It was often about possession, about marking territory, about impulse. She thought that Baptiste did not want to be the kind of man who marked territory.

He was quiet. Then he said, I am sorry. For kissing you.

I didn't mind, she said. It was the assumption. Ask me next time.

And as she said this, she wondered if he would ask her right then, Can I kiss you?

But he didn't ask.

Can I say something? he said.

Of course.

I like you, Lucille. And I think that you like me. But I am young, and you are older. But that shouldn't matter, should it? But to you it does matter. Or something matters. I watch you, and you are like the horse that is afraid to jump over the fence. You approach at full gallop and then suddenly stop, and your rider goes over the fence, but you stay on this side. You know? Do you think that is right?

Oh, Baptiste. You should do psychological profiles.

But you haven't answered my question. Is that right?

Are you the rider that goes over the fence? she asked.

Ha, see? Once again. Is that right?

It's not so simple.

But it is. Either you are afraid to jump the fence, or you aren't.

No, Baptiste. I can jump the fence. But not with you.

But of course, he was right. She was afraid to jump the fence. Afraid to choose. But that wasn't completely right either, because she was choosing. Just not what he wanted.

If not me, he said, then who?

There might be someone out there. An older man. An uglier man. A stupider man. But not a young boy like you.

But there is no other man. Not in this moment. Why are you waiting for the older, stupider, uglier one?

She closed her eyes. Opened them. She looked at Baptiste, and he did not look away. She said, In a perfect world, I would choose differently.

So you are waiting for the perfect world, he said. And then he said that he would tell her about his mother. He hadn't talked about his mother for a long time. Not with anyone. But he would tell Lucille. He said that every Sunday night, his mother used to prepare a paella for the family. Chicken fried in oil. Sliced chorizo and pancetta and onion, garlic and parsley stalks. Stock and peas, prawns, mussels, and squid. Rice and saffron and lemon. As he described the dish, his hands moved about.

She waited.

He said that his mother's name was Claudette. She was an architect. She had built many beautiful buildings. She had designed and built the family summer house near Uzès, in the country, northeast of Montpellier. One weekend, about two years ago, she had gone up to spend time there, and when she did not return, the children had become worried and Baptiste drove out to the house. His father was out of the picture, he had a new wife and a young child, and he was not involved in Claudette's life. In front of the house, there was a small lake, and there was a rowboat, and Baptiste said that when he arrived, he found the rowboat floating in the middle of the lake. His mother was not to be found. When her body was finally discovered at the bottom of the small lake, it was determined that she had drowned. Which was very strange, because she had been a good swimmer, and when they studied her body, there was nothing to indicate a bump on the head, or a heart attack. He didn't believe she had killed herself. His sisters thought she had. His father as well, though his father's voice in the whole matter meant nothing. *Absolument rien.* Of course, his mother had not been happy. Her business was not doing well. She was lonely. He had often asked her if she needed him. He could come over if she liked, in the evening, or on weekends. She always said no. He loved her. She loved him. They had always been close. He hadn't thought that her behaviour was odd, or that her depression was serious.

Some people were just melancholic. They liked to be left alone. That was his mother. He didn't think she would leave him. Why would a mother leave her children?

Lucille saw his hand on his thigh, and she imagined taking it, and holding it, but she didn't, because she didn't know if that would make him stop talking, and she didn't want him to stop talking.

It must have been difficult, she said. Going to the summer house to find her.

I didn't find her. The police did. But I knew she was gone. Under the water. When I climbed out of the car, her dog was on the dock, pacing and barking. She would not stop. And so, I knew. Even so, I ran from the house and back to the dock and back to the house, calling her name. She didn't leave a note. This is why I think it was an accident. Do you agree?

I can't know, Baptiste.

I don't understand. I would never do that to a child of mine. Kill myself without explaining.

She must have suffered.

For a year, I was angry. I am still angry. Though with you, I am not angry. You are the only one.

Lucille was quiet.

He said that his father was emotionless. His sisters were remote. One had a daughter.

Lucille said that that was so lovely. He was lucky to be an uncle.

On a previous Friday, they had named themselves as objects in the world. The trick was to name the first thing that came to mind. Don't overthink it.

He had been a boat.

She asked why a boat.

At first, he couldn't say.

A boat floats, she said.

Or sinks.

A lifeboat, she said.

A big boat? she asked. A ship?

He said that it was small. It fit one or two.

She said that that was sufficient.

He said that it could take water and capsize.

And you can bail, she had said.

And now, when he spoke of his mother, she saw that of course a boat. Nothing but a boat.

That night, he stayed and slept in her guest room. She couldn't sleep. She was listening for him, for his breathing, for any movement that might suggest that he was looking for her, that he would enter her room and lie down beside her. In the morning, she walked up to the bakery and bought croissants that he refused to eat because they were not true croissants. He peeled an orange and ate it slowly. After, when he was gone, pushed out by her into the fresh snow, she cleaned up the kitchen and she went upstairs and made the guest bed. She smelled his pillow. She had never spoken to him of Martin, and his death. The opportunity had been there, the night before, but death was not a competition. And so, he did not know. And she would not tell him.

——

DAVID BERGEN

All that week, her mind was in disarray. She was irritated
with her patients. Their difficulties seemed petty. On Friday,
he called as she was preparing pizza. He said that something
had come up. *Désolé*. She said that it was no problem. She
told him to have a good evening. She ate alone.

And then one day the following week, driving through
downtown on an errand, she saw a boy who looked like
Baptiste walking hand in hand with a girl. They were
laughing. Talking. Their gait was jaunty and easy and full
of life, and in the cold of the day, their breath passed out
of their mouths and lifted upwards. She passed them by
and glanced at the couple and she saw that it was indeed
Baptiste. With that little girl. From the wedding. She pulled
the car to the curb. Watched as Baptiste and the girl entered
a coffee shop. They ordered. Sat at a table by the window.
Baptiste was talking, moving his hands here and there as
he did when he was excited. The girl laughed and threw
her head back and then touched Baptiste's face. Lucille
started her car and pulled away from the curb and out into
the street. She felt happy for him. She felt devastated. She
saw her face in the rear-view mirror and said, You old hag.

For the remainder of the day, she felt as if she had
slipped sideways, as if someone had come along and gently
but firmly planted a hand on her shoulder and shoved her
slightly. Not hard enough to fall, but enough to wobble.
She was alone on a large rock in the middle of an ocean.
She did not put out any SOS. She did not slip a note into
a bottle and send it out to sea. She did not wave at passing
ships; rather, she hid when the ships appeared on the
horizon.

He did not call or text. And she did not contact him. He simply disappeared. And now that he was gone, she began to speak of him. She told Dr. Helguson about Baptiste.

Dr. Helguson said, So, you found love again.

You're not going to berate me? Lucille asked.

I think you're doing a good enough job of that.

I'm such a fool. I'm ashamed. I imagine him laughing at me. Telling that little tart about this grandma that he used and then abandoned.

You are a grandma.

I was more than a grandma, certainly.

But you want it to be about the age difference. And the impossibility. And that you were used. And your moral backbone. Why not just say that there was love?

He was so sweet. And lovely. And kind. And lost. I should have told him about Martin. I'm sorry now that I didn't go out with him in public and hold his hand, so that everyone could see that I was alive and lucky, and they would all say, Look at that, isn't Lucille Black something? Which is ironic, given that I laughed at Morris when he paraded around with his young women. That desperate need to feel potent. Which is a wonderful feeling. I always thought it was a male thing, running from death. Boy, did I get a lesson. I don't know what to do. My brain is scattered. I'm doing poorly at my job. I'm out of place. Oh, fuck. I pushed him away.

You make it sound like you decided everything. That you chose for him.

Can you imagine if others had known? How they would have laughed at me?

119

And so, you keep hiding.

It's private. My life. My leap off the deep end.

You spend so much time hiding and worrying about being caught, Lucille, that you can't even catch yourself. Take a look. Or have you forgotten how to look? I'm not here to handhold. If you want that, you can go up the street to one of those therapists with a diploma from a local community college.

And she was dismissed.

Two weeks later, he texted her. Formally, as if this were a letter.

Chère Lucille, I'm sorry for being absent. I took your counsel and have found a friend. Her name is Mel. She is a dancer. You would like her mind. It is healthy. I would love to introduce you to her sometime. But I understand if you don't want that. Avec amour, Baptiste.

She wrote back within the day.

Baptiste. I would love to meet Mel, if you are still willing. Do let me know. Lucille.

She did not write, *Love, Lucille.* She did not say, *With love.* She had been absolutely authentic in her offer. She wanted to meet Mel. She wanted to see Baptiste again. They met at a Vietnamese restaurant on a Saturday evening in late December. It was crowded and hot in the restaurant. Lucille was early. She found a table and sat facing the door and removed her coat. She was wearing a long-sleeved sweater. Her hair was pulled back. She ordered tea. She waited. Fifteen minutes. Half an hour. She began to gather her coat with a feeling of relief when she saw them outside on the sidewalk. He had his arm around her shoulder. And then he removed it. The little girl entered first and stepped sideways. Baptiste swung in, his scarf trailing him, his gestures expansive. He came to Lucille and pulled her to her feet and kissed her on each cheek and whispered that she was beautiful, and he was so happy. Lucille pushed Baptiste back gently and held out a hand to the waiting girl.

Mel was shy and tentative and soft, and she ate almost nothing. She was constantly touching Baptiste. His hair, his forearm, his cheek. Holding his hand when it was free. Brushing stray food from his lip. She listened to Baptiste and Lucille talk, and when she had something to say, she said it so softly that Lucille had to ask her to repeat herself. Baptiste was tender with her. He called her *ma petite*. Lucille noticed Mel's hands, and her skin, and her beautiful eyes, which studied Lucille as if checking her out. Lucille found herself doing the math in her head. She realized that Mel was at least forty years younger than she was, and this was so extreme as to be humorous. What did Baptiste want? What game was he playing? Such attention he paid to Mel, trying so hard. And she saw for the first time that he was weak. How had she not seen that before? Immediately, she was sorry for this thought, and she tried to engage Mel, in order to make her comfortable, but it was not easy. It was only when she asked about dance that Mel lifted her head and spoke with confidence, and Lucille saw what Baptiste must have seen: a girl who was very naive and who was more in touch with her body than her mind. Of course. Lucille's heart opened. When they said goodbye, she hugged Mel and whispered that she had found a wonderful young man, good for her, and Mel whispered back, I know. Baptiste kissed Lucille, as was his habit, and she said, See you again, though she believed that this would not be the case.

And then, a few months later, he reached her by phone. It was a weekday evening, and she was sitting by the fire, reading. She recognized his number, and she considered not answering, but then she did answer finally, and she was not sorry. He was crying. He said that he was alone. Could he come see her?

She said that it was late. She was working tomorrow.

I am alone, he said again. Mel has left me. He asked if he could come.

She said yes.

It was one of the coldest nights of the year, and she imagined him trudging to the bus stop and waiting and waiting in his thin coat and his ever-present scarf. She could call him back and offer to pick him up, but she resisted. Let him come on his own. She went upstairs and changed. She had already washed her face for the night, but now she sat before her vanity and put on fresh makeup and fixed her hair, and she wore a necklace that he liked, and she wore jeans and a button-down white shirt, and when she saw herself, she laughed and removed the white shirt and put on an old T-shirt. And then changed back to the white shirt. Her hands were shaking. Stop it, she said. Stay in place. But what place was that?

He came, and she let him in, and he held her. In the foyer. His thin coat and a yellow scarf and no hat. His poor ears. She pressed her hands against his ears and said that he was a foolish boy and why didn't he get a toque.

He was timid at first, and the tears he'd offered her on the phone were gone now. She took his coat and threw it over the railing of the staircase. She told him to sit by the fire and warm himself. She went into the kitchen and boiled water for tea, and when she came back to the living room, he was in a chair by the fire. He looked up.

Thank you, he said.

Of course, she said, but she wasn't sure what that meant. Of course he was thankful? Of course she would be here? Of course they would pick up where they had left off?

She sat down on the couch, away from him.

I hurt you, he said. I'm sorry.

You didn't hurt me.

He was surprised. Maybe disappointed.

Perhaps I hurt you, she said. I didn't think about what you needed.

I wanted you, he said.

She smiled. She asked what had happened, with Mel.

She said that you were always in the room. In the bed. Lucille this. Lucille that. She told me to go back to you.

And here you are.

Here I am.

What do you want, Baptiste?

He said, I told Mel about our conversations, about how we talked, not the topics, but the way in which we talked, and I guess I said that I wanted that with her, but she didn't know what I meant, or how to talk. Not like you. She was shallow, or maybe she was just too young, and she didn't understand words. I wanted her to fight back. I wanted to argue with her. To discuss. And she said, You want me to be Lucille. If you want another mother, go back to her.

Maybe she was right.

Do you think so?

I don't know. All I know is that you are a bit lost, and that you are looking for someone, perhaps it is your mother, whatever that means. I don't know what your mother meant to you, really. Or what your childhood was like. I know none of this.

It's strange, he said, but I always saw my mother as utilitarian. I loved her, yes, but she was like a fixture, in the kitchen, in the home, at her work, thinking, drawing, over there. And then she died, and when I try to conjure up images of her, or memories, they are faint, and vague. She is a shadow. And I feel bad for not remembering her more clearly. Though I ache when I think of the paella, for example, or when I go up to the house in Uzès, and I know that she designed it and had it built, and I want her to be there still, but she isn't. That is when I feel a great emptiness.

Lucille said that the emptiness would come and go. And with each passing year, it would feel less overwhelming, and it would be less frightening. You don't believe me, I can see, but it is true. This will happen.

—

Baptiste disappeared from her life. Only to reappear a year later in the form of a letter, requesting her attendance at the celebration of his marriage to Inèz, to be held in Uzès, France, in August. Lucille felt something, but she couldn't locate it. Maybe jealousy. Or sadness. Or offence. Wistfulness. Or it might be happiness. Strange that she didn't know what she felt. She, of all people, should know. She put the invitation aside with no plans to attend. She would write a little note and congratulate them. Wish the couple a happy life. Everyone should have a happy life.

And then, a few days later, in the middle of the night and suffering insomnia, the windows to her bedroom wide open, allowing in the sounds that brought great comfort — a train crossing the bridge at Omand's Creek, a plane taxiing at the airport, sirens bleeding into the sky, a cat howling — she realized that she had no plans for August. She did not see patients during that month and so she had nothing. Baptiste had slipped a note into the invitation, in which he had said that he would love to see her at the wedding. Her presence there would mean much. He would like to show her the house at Uzès and introduce her to his fiancée. And his sisters. He would save a little room for her, upstairs, where there was a window that overlooked the lake. August was the most beautiful time. It was going to be a grand party. Come celebrate with us, he said. And he signed off, *Avec amour*.

If she said yes, would she be running from her life here? Perhaps. And running towards a different life? Doubtful. She was wise enough to understand that wherever she ran to, she would still be taking Lucille Black with her.

She resurrected Michel Thomas, and at night, when she could not sleep, she worked on various tenses. For example, the perfect continuous conditional, in which there was always some implication of regret, of something unfulfilled—If I had known, I wouldn't have come.

Finally, in the third week of July, she wrote Baptiste.

J'arrive, she said.

At night, in the hotel room whose windows overlooked the lights of Phuket, Lucille dreamed that she was having sex with Shane. Or, about to. She was getting undressed and tossing her clothes here and there. At one point, she was in her underwear, with only high heels on her feet, and the shoes pinched and hurt. She bent to remove them and found that they would not come off. She sat on the bed, amongst the pile of clothes, breathless now because Shane was ready and waiting for her. And her anxiety at being sloppy and unprepared turned into shame that became actual shame when she woke.

She was shivering. The air conditioning was on high. She climbed from the bed, careful not to disrupt Libby beside her, and she turned the air conditioning down. A lower hum now. She went out onto the balcony and looked down at the city. Her body had been highly tuned, ready for him, and she realized that she was still in a frenzy, and more so because she had wanted him. Something so pitched that it still felt real. And why? As often happened in dreams, she at first made it about the facts, and was humiliated. Sex with a pretender. And with desire. But a desire for what? To be him? To have what he had? Which was the attention of Libby? And what better way to throw Libby off the trail than to take what Libby wanted. And to become Shane.

And in that way, she could have it every which way. And save herself. And save her daughter.

She still suffered dreams of lateness. She was late for an appointment—her hair, one of her patients, a movie—and on each occasion, she knew that someone else had taken her place, and she could hear the hairdresser talking to that someone, and she heard the psychiatrist, who wasn't her, offering comfort to that someone, and she heard the film playing and a whole bunch of someones laughing and enjoying the film. But she wasn't there. She hadn't made it. She wasn't anyone. And she wasn't there.

Breathlessness. Panic. She felt that now. She stepped inside and rummaged through her bag for a pack of cigarettes. She stepped outside. The smoke in her lungs was a comfort. She didn't smoke in front of Libby. None of her patients knew she smoked. She hid it from everyone. So there you go. Lucille hiding. But she liked hiding. She was like a shoplifter who steals not for the object but for the pleasure of the chance that she might be caught. And then not being caught. The object—a scarf, a frying pan, makeup—meant nothing. It was the sense of knowledge. I know something—you don't.

Take Baptiste. No one had known. Save for Juan, and Dr. Helguson, who were both bound by the codes of their profession. Long ago, Lucille had taken an English class in which they read a story about a Russian man who has an affair with a young woman, and at supper one night, with a friend, the Russian tells the friend about the lovely young woman he has met, wanting to say more. The friend's response? Yes, the fish was a bit off, wasn't it? For

Lucille, that line had been the most poignant of the story. She wasn't interested in stories for structure or emotional crescendo. She was aroused by the smaller details, the manner in which friends ignored each other, or did not listen, or when a character like the Russian wanted to describe the passion he had experienced with his lover, but the friend dismissed him. Perhaps out of jealousy. Or lack of interest. Or revenge. Or perhaps it was as Libby had said: people were only interested in themselves.

Except for parents, who forsook themselves for the children. She would be a mother until she died, and her children would always be her children. Even when Lucille was seventy-five, and Libby was forty-five, Libby would still wield control over her.

∞

The boat to Phi Phi was smaller than the boat in the photograph they had been shown when they bought their tickets the day before. The boat in the picture had been grand, with two decks, and it had a capacity for two hundred people, and there were lifeboats and it looked safe. This boat was small, and as the passengers were embarking, Lucille saw that there were far too many people for such a small vessel. She complained immediately. She said, This is not the right boat. We bought tickets for a bigger boat. A safer boat.

The young boy who was helping the passengers board shrugged and said in English that he did not speak English. Sorry.

Lucille stood to gather her bag. She told Libby she wasn't going.

Mom, don't. This is embarrassing. It'll be fine. Relax.

And Lucille listened. She sat down. She looked for a life jacket, and when she couldn't see any, she asked the boy for one. She mimed putting on a life jacket and he grinned at her and said, No problem. There was one couple arguing about whether or not to stay on the boat, but for the most part, the other passengers were easygoing and seemingly oblivious, and this being so, she tried to stifle her anxiety and fear. Why should she always be the one to see danger where there wasn't any?

The small boat, low in the water, laboured out of the harbour and into the open sea. The sun shone brilliantly, reflecting off the calm water, which was azure and reminded one of the pictures in travel brochures where a young couple, he muscular, she in a tiny bathing suit, both with brilliant teeth, cavort and laugh. Birds followed the boat, climbing high into the sky and then plummeting with great speed towards the water. She relaxed. Around them, the chatter of many languages. A young man sat close to Libby and told her where in Holland he lived, and he told her that he was travelling alone, and he said that he had an open ticket and he had no intention of returning home soon. They spoke of the various islands in the gulf, and he talked about a music festival he wanted to attend, and Libby said she might go there as well. Lucille, who was pretending not to listen, thought this was impossible if Libby was going to be with Shane. Lucille found herself dreaming. Libby would become attached to the Dutchman, and then fall in love, and she would go to the music festival and of course ingest all types of drugs, and party till the morning, but anything would be better than the cult of Shane. She was lulled by the sound of the voices, and by the hope of Libby and the Dutchman, and she became drowsy and closed her eyes briefly.

When she opened her eyes, the boat had acquired a different rhythm. It was rising and falling. Behind them, the sky was darker, and the water around them was darker, and the waves were higher. And then it began to rain, and the passengers ducked their heads, and some put on rain gear. The wind grew. The boat sank into deep furrows and then rose high on the sea, so that at the peak of the wave, one could see the angry ocean, and feel the furious wind. The birds had disappeared.

Many of the passengers were now worried. Some called out for life jackets, but the boy was gone. The captain kept turning to look backwards at the approaching storm. A young couple near Lucille, with two young children, toddlers, clutched at each other and their children. An older man threw up over the side. And when the force of the storm hit, a cry went up and people began to scream. The Dutchman was stoic. He asked Libby if she could swim. Yes. And your mother? Yes. He told the young couple that if they needed help with their children, he would do so. He was a strong swimmer.

In the depths of the trough of a wave, there was nothing to see but the blackness of the angry water, and as the boat rose slowly, its engine straining, and they reached the height of a wave, there was nothing to see but the rain and the black water and the bottom of the wave far below, into which they slid sideways. Libby held Lucille's hand. The other clutched at the Dutchman's large hand. She said that they were going to die. Lucille said that it would be fine, though she didn't feel this. They would die. All around her, passengers wept and threw up and cried out. Incredible. She hated always being right, and yet she had been right once again — to not trust this boat, or the skipper, or the boy. And now everyone would suffer the consequences of her rightness, of her vision of disaster. Fucking stupid country. Stupid her. Stupid boy who said, No problem. She wanted Libby to live. She didn't care about herself.

If we capsize, she told Libby, don't worry about your things. No shoes. No bags. Keep your head above water, and don't try to save anyone.

The Dutchman put his arms around Libby and she pressed her face against his chest. He was a tall and muscular man, not more than twenty-five years old, and he could have carried three Libbys on his back, or in his arms. He was impassive. It's good, he said. It was like a film, Lucille thought. A script had been written and now it was being played out.

The boat shuddered. In fact, the boat groaned. Lucille heard it, and then realized that it was the collective groan of the passengers, for a groan in every language is a common noise. Universal incomprehensibility.

She thought about the novel she had not yet finished reading, and she was sorry, for she wanted to know what would become of the narrator. And then realized that she knew what would become of her. She would have heard a few more confessions from strangers, or acquaintances, and she would have registered no outright judgment at people's choices or beliefs or stories, and she would make an occasional reference to her children at home, whom she seemed to rarely see but obviously loved, witnessed in the phone calls that came her way late at night, or midday, and the story would end not in death at sea, or in death in any way, for it was not a story about violent death, but it was a story about knowledge.

And so, should they go overboard, the book would stay in her bag, with her passport and credit cards and bathing suit and the dress she had brought along for Baptiste's wedding. She wanted this to be done. Either go over, or survive.

And then, as if a tap had been turned off, the rain stopped, and the waves lessened, and the sun came out, and the boat slipped into the sheltered side of an island and the passengers cheered. The captain slowed the boat and came to rest near a shoal where the coral below was brilliant and brilliant fish swam beside the boat, and it was the brilliant Dutchman who was first in the water, for the captain had invited those who wanted to swim, to swim, there were masks available, and then Libby pulled off her dress and was now down to her underwear, and she was over the side as well, and then others, all those who could swim.

Lucille wanted to swim, but she didn't have a bathing suit at hand, and she certainly couldn't change on the boat, and she wouldn't fall into the water in only underwear, which was a privilege of youth and perfection. She leaned forward and dipped her hand into the water. Touched the water to her face.

Half of the passengers were now overboard. Even the old man who had been throwing up over the gunnel was dog-paddling about, his grey head bobbing, his flat forehead and snubbed nose resembling the features of a small shark. The Dutchman was swimming with long strokes, head buried, back rippling. Lucille admired him. Thought him a god. Take my daughter. Who was wearing a mask, facing the ocean floor, floating like a dead woman, her whitish-grey underwear suctioned to her body. Coming up for air. Going under again. Until the captain called out, and the swimmers turned back to the boat. When the last of them had clambered back on, the engine fired up and the boat chugged from the harbour and towards the shores of Phi Phi.

∞

When she was twenty-one and in university, Libby had a relationship with a professor who was twenty years her senior. At the time — still lost in the fog of Martin's death — Lucille had just left Morris and was having her own affair with the heart surgeon. Either Lucille was unaware of Libby's relationship, or she chose to ignore it, or her mind went simple. It was Morris who became involved in Libby's life. He made threats, sent letters, pushed notes under office doors, and eventually cornered the professor. He was being Morris — passionate, angry, protective, and invasive. Lucille loved that about him. And, of course, hated it. His extreme loyalty. His desire to be right. His need to be needed. His acting out. His rage. His moral indignation. His sadness. His love.

What little bits Lucille knew about Libby's affair came to her via Morris, for it was to Morris that Libby turned when she wanted a confessor. And a soft heart. The professor was married. In fact, his wife was pregnant. In fact, the day after the birth of this professor's child, Libby went to him, or he to her, and they holed up in a hotel room, and then they went out into the Exchange, shopping for a piece of jewellery for this professor's wife, a gift, and Libby helped to choose this gift. When Morris passed on all of this information to Lucille, Lucille was furious. Why are you having these conversations with our daughter? That is private. She shouldn't be offering her father details from her sexual life. Don't tell me any more of this. I don't want to know.

Oh Christ, Lucille, Morris said. For one who claims to face the facts, you do the opposite. This is Libby asking for help with a rapist professor. At least I'm doing something.

The affair did not last. The professor left Libby, who was devastated, and then the professor returned and chased after Libby for half a year until Morris once again got involved and threatened him with all types of grim consequences. Libby didn't seem to mind that her father inserted himself into her life. She forgave him his nosiness, saw it as affection. She treated him as if he might break. Not so, her mother. Libby was very hard on Lucille, as if Libby saw in Lucille her future self, and didn't like what she saw.

∾

In the afternoon, after settling into their bungalow, which gave out onto the beach, they found a space on the sand and laid out towels and swam and drank coconut milk and read and swam some more. They did little talking. Lucille finished her book and deemed it worthwhile, even though it hadn't truly ended. Not in the manner of a traditional story. It left swaths of room for the narration to expand and go any which way. Nothing resolved, save the resolution of life going on and on. Until one died. Though there had been no mention of death. But she had smelled it.

Libby spent hours on her phone. Scrolling and tapping. More scrolling. Rolling from her back to her stomach. Asking Lucille to spread on another layer of suntan lotion, which she did, loving to touch her daughter's soft skin. Such strong legs. Still so young. She was wearing a two-piece. The dress had been tucked away somewhere, and Lucille hoped it would stay tucked away.

The phone was surprising. In Pattaya, Libby had been so dismissive of anything to do with technology. It made her angry. It was competitive. It was the thief of happiness. And now, here she was, sliding down the hole of her phone.

Who are you talking to? Lucille asked at one point.

A long silence. Then, Friends.

Which friends?

Old. New.

Lucille watched a family walk down the beach. A mother, a father, and two daughters. The mother was topless, as were the young girls, and the father was wearing a Speedo. They passed by. They were speaking French.

The sun was setting. It was nearing five in the afternoon. They shared a piece of watermelon purchased from a passing vendor. Lucille stood and went down to the water and washed her hands. She rose. She stretched. She came back to Libby, who was watching her.

You look great, Mama.

Not sure about that, Lucille said.

You do. Believe me.

Lucille was pleased. But she hid her pleasure. She reached into her bag and took out her cigarettes. Lit one. Blew the smoke up into the air. It's a holiday, she said. I like one now and then on my holidays.

Libby smiled. I don't care, Mom. I know that you smoke.

Do you?

Oh, Mama, you're so funny. I'm going dancing tonight with Cees.

Who?

Cees, the Dutchman that you were admiring on the boat.

When did you arrange that?

Just now.

Okay. Fine. But we can have dinner together?

Yes. I'm starving.

∽

At night, a storm threw rain against the open windows and onto the foot of Lucille's bed and woke her. She climbed out from the mosquito net and closed the shutters. Libby's bed was still empty. She checked the time: 3 a.m. She climbed back under the mosquito net and lay listening to the rain and the thunder. She checked her phone. Nothing from Libby. She wouldn't sleep now. This she knew.

At dinner, Lucille had had many things to say, but deemed them unworthy, or if not unworthy, then risky. Of course, she hoped that Libby would come to her senses and never go back to that awful compound where girls walked around like they were acting out a scene from *The Handmaid's Tale.* How was it possible that her daughter, whom she had raised to be an independent woman, had fallen for a man who was a scoundrel and a quack? The whole scene was a horror. The bare rooms, the lack of food, the filth, the dresses, the braids, the silent peeling of potatoes, the simplistic notion of recovery, the patriarchy, the sexual heaviness.

But she said nothing of this. Instead, they both exclaimed about the food — whole fish that had been fried in garlic, and a spicy cucumber salad, and a potato and chicken curry.

Lucille said that she was excited for Libby. It would be fun with the Dutchman. She asked how to spell his name.

Libby told her.

I would pronounce that *cease*, Lucille said.

The language is guttural. Hard consonants. Cees said it's like you are clearing your throat.

He's lovely, Lucille said.

It won't work, Mom. Though he is lovely. And kind. You think that I am not thinking.

You're an incredible thinker. Though I think Shane has done something to you. I worry about the dressing up.

We all dress up. Did you see that French family today? On the beach? They were playing at dressing up. Or undressing. It's only the body. We make too much of the body. And women's breasts. And nakedness.

They shared a tapioca dessert. Lucille had a soft spot for any kind of dessert, and Libby knew this, and so Libby ordered it, telling her mother that she would love this. It was special. And Lucille found it so. After her final bite of the dessert, Libby said that she was going to go back to the bungalow and change. Cees would be waiting for her.

The rain, when it halted, stopped so quickly that it seemed someone had put up a sheet or a mammoth piece of plywood to dam the onslaught. And then, a few minutes later, there were voices, a man and a woman's, and outside on the verandah there were footsteps, and the voices stopped, and for a long time it was quiet, though there was the occasional whisper of a voice, tender, inquiring, and then silence again. And the rustle of feet. And then Libby was inside the bungalow, undressing, climbing under the mosquito net. Lucille saw her in the shadows. Saw her body. Saw her pull her hair back and then slide into bed. She wanted to speak. To ask her if she was fine. What desires she felt. What she was thinking. Where she was going. When this uncertainty would end. Whether she loved her. If she was still angry. If she was forgiven. If she would ever be forgiven. But she said nothing, and Libby fell asleep quickly, her breathing so slow and so easy. And for a moment, Lucille believed that Libby was a baby again, and Lucille had succeeded in putting her down, and now she would creep from the room and leave her for the night. She would go back to herself but keep an ear open. Just in case.

Libby slept a lot that week. She ate breakfast late, large plates of food that she first admired, took a photo of, and then devoured. Lucille, who had been up at first light and had completed what felt like a whole day, sat across from her and drank a smoothie, typically pineapple and mango and banana. She watched her daughter eat. Sometimes Cees joined them. He was easygoing and gregarious and he had a large laugh, too loud perhaps, but that was compensated for by his avidity for life. He and Libby spent the evenings together, and perhaps the nights as well, though Lucille did not ask, but it was typical that Libby came in just before dawn, and slept late, and Lucille assumed that Libby had been with Cees. So be it. The Dutch were good people. They knew how to build dams, and they preferred bicycles over cars, and they didn't use window coverings, and to Lucille's mind, this was an indication of a people who were open, and fair, and industrious, people who had nothing to hide. And yet were full of respect. She secretly wished that Libby would announce that she had fallen in love with Cees, and that she would be returning to Holland with him, and that they were planning a spring wedding. Or just planning. Something. Anything.

Cees had an older brother who worked in film. His parents were both teachers. He was still trying to understand what he might be. These were his words. He was a carpenter and was taking a year off to travel. His next stop was Cambodia, where he planned to meet his brother. He said that he was leaving the island the following morning. This was on Libby and Lucille's fourth night on the island. Libby seemed more settled. She had begun to read again. Trashy novels that she'd found in the café where she ate her large breakfasts. Her skin was ripening, and her face was filling out.

When Cees said that he would be leaving, Libby had seemed unperturbed. Lucille was surprised, and perhaps she showed the surprise, because she said that they would miss him.

Cees smiled and said that he usually stayed in a place for three days, and then he became restless. He said that, as a little boy, he could never sit still. At school, he was always being sent from the room because he was disruptive. Too much curiosity. Sticking a fork into an electrical outlet, just to see, or disturbing the hamster in the cage, setting it loose into the room. It was always more interesting to do what was not allowed, because if it was not allowed, there must be something special behind the no. He was averse to the word *no*. His mother learned quite quickly to say yes to everything, with an explanation. This did not stop him from, for example, sewing a parachute and jumping from a second-storey window onto the street below. He broke his arm. Got a concussion. But it was worth it, because he learned that you need more height in order for the wind to catch the parachute. Now he jumped from ten thousand feet, with a real parachute. He put his hand on Libby's shoulder blade and moved it back and forth.

He wore a muscle shirt that advertised a Thai hot sauce, and he wore shorts that were very short, and his legs were tanned and long, and his jaw was honest, which was Lucille's interpretation — this meant that he was not weak-looking, like that cult leader Shane. Cees could never be a guru, he was too concrete, too in love with the physical world, too in love with the appearance of the body. He was constantly reaching out to Libby, and she didn't seem to mind. Appeared to like it, in fact. And she reciprocated. They sometimes held hands between courses, and Lucille found this lovely. But what meaning to make of it? He was leaving tomorrow, and Libby would be without distractions. This worried Lucille.

Cees paid attention to Lucille. He asked her questions, and he listened to her answers. He said that Lucille reminded him of his own mother, who was a bit of a worrier, but that was what mothers had to do, didn't they, and if children didn't have mothers, where would they be? His mother made great homemade pasta, and she made a potato dish with cheese that had been his favourite as a boy. Sometimes, when he'd been living in his own apartment, and he needed a recipe, he'd call up his mother and ask her for the details, and she would be so pleased to give it to him. His mother wasn't just domestic, she taught full-time, young children of seven and eight, but it was cooking for her boys that was ultimate. And hearing their voices on the phone. He said that he didn't call his mother often enough. In fact, tonight he would send her an email, just to make her happy. She loved hearing about his trip, and he didn't make enough contact. It was easy to take a mother for granted, especially if she was permanent and faithful. I love her. But I don't miss her. Not like she misses me.

How do you know that she misses you? Lucille asked. Maybe she's happy to have you happy, and she doesn't need daily reminders.

Cees said that this was possible, but not probable. My father sends me notes, or he reminds me to call my mother. And I do that. Because she is my mother.

Lucille hoped that Libby was listening to all of this. She wondered how much Libby had told Cees about her life. About Lucille's life. About anything. He would be wise. He would have straight answers.

The following afternoon, on the beach, Libby was quiet. Cees had left early. Libby had been sleeping when Cees climbed onto the boat and trawled out of the harbour. Lucille had gone down to the dock to say goodbye. Cees had seemed surprised to see her, almost embarrassed, and this had created some consternation in Lucille, who wondered if she had overstepped some sort of boundary, but then Cees had recovered, and he'd hugged her for a long time, and she had noticed his size, and his strength, and his generosity. He pulled back from her and he said that she had raised a beautiful daughter and that she should be proud. Don't worry about her, he said. She was surprised at his adamance, almost as if he were speaking for Libby, but she threw aside her doubts and touched his arm and said, Thank you. And she said his name, and knew immediately that she had mispronounced it, for he smiled, and touched her arm, and walked away.

They would never see each other again. This was
the nature of travelling — meeting strangers, becoming
intimate with them, and then saying goodbye. The end.
She had had a few experiences of this type, at conferences,
and one time when young, travelling through the Maritimes
alone, she had met an older couple who had befriended
her for two days, and perhaps because of the anonymity,
she had given herself over to them, and then they'd said
goodbye, and Lucille had asked if they could exchange
contact information, but the couple either had not heard
her or ignored her, and Lucille had been slightly hurt and
wondered what the last few days had meant to them, if
anything, and so that had been her first experience of
brief intimacy and then departure, and so she knew that,
in most people's lives, this was common and acceptable,
and perhaps it was because of her independent nature, and
her reluctance to reveal herself, that when she did finally
bare herself, she expected something more lasting.

It was the off-season, and the sun was intermittent, and it rained often, and this forced them to take shelter beneath the bamboo roof of a bar or a café, where the music was loud, and it was difficult to hear the other person speaking. Without Cees as a buffer, they became impatient and short with each other. To avoid this, Lucille took long walks down the beach, past young people sprawled on the sand, stopping at a restaurant for a bite to eat, and then returning in the late afternoon to find Libby playing paddleball with some stranger, or floating in the water, or sleeping in the bungalow, curled up on her bed, the fan lifting the few loose tendrils of hair that had escaped her braids. For she had gone back to braiding her hair. Sometimes two braids, sometimes a single braid, and, once, a crown braid that revealed her jaw and her long neck and was, if chosen and not commanded, quite beautiful. Lucille, in her darker moments, saw the braids as a sign that Libby would go back. She was preparing herself, and there was nothing Lucille could say or do.

One night, Lucille woke in a sweat. The electricity was off, and the fan was quiet, and it was completely dark. No music from the nearby bar. A few voices on the beach. She removed her sheet cover, climbed from the bed, put on shorts and a T-shirt, and stepped outside onto the verandah. Waves, small and regular, fell against the shore and receded and then came back. She stepped down off the porch and took the path towards the beach. She stood at the water's edge and looked out at the dark outlines of the limestone cliffs. Farther down the beach, someone had built a bonfire, and there were figures moving back and forth and here and there, and from her point of view, it seemed a scene from a time long past, primitive and embryonic, and the occasional cries that rose from the group were like the calls of warriors preparing for a hunt. She was no longer enjoying herself. She felt greedy, crude, misanthropic. All these bodies. Hers included. She found herself watching Libby too closely, studying how she walked, the clothes she chose, how she talked to strange men in a restaurant or on the beach, her flirting, and her smile, which turned to irritation whenever she faced her mother. Where had this come from? Wisely, she chose to ignore the irritation. She became softer with Libby.

She had brought with her from Canada a hair colouring kit, and on the last day, she asked Libby if she would colour her hair. Libby agreed. Lucille sat on a chair on the verandah while Libby prepared the kit. She put on gloves. Asked Lucille to hold the container with the mix. Libby stood behind her, and with every movement, Lucille felt her body, and heard her breathing. Libby was very gentle, she took her time. Lucille said how grateful she was, and Libby said that it was nothing.

Lucille said that it wasn't nothing. Martin used to colour her hair. He loved it. She didn't know why, but he got a kick out of it.

Maybe he liked being close to you. You did love him.

Lucille said that she loved all her children equally. It was just that Martin was loud. He asked for a lot.

I didn't? Libby asked.

No. You were in the shadows. You chose that. You were always like that. Not wanting interference. Making your own way. You still are.

Libby asked if Lucille was excited to see Baptiste.

You could come with me, Lucille said. He told me to bring someone.

To France.

Yes.

That would be perfect. For you. Let's play a game. Capture Libby.

I don't want to capture you.

Libby said that, before she ended up in Pattaya, she had met a man from Italy named Guido. They travelled northern Thailand together. She said that Guido's family owned a farm in the Alto Adige valley, in the Alps, wine country, and he was taking six months to travel before settling down. He was thirty-five. She said that Guido joined her at the compound originally, but only lasted two days. He had political views. Quite strong. And those views were contrary to Shane's. She said that Lucille would have liked him. The two of them would have seen eye to eye. She sounded wistful.

And you just let him go? This boy?

He wasn't a boy. And I didn't let him go. He left. He thought the whole business there was crazy. He hated the control.

You hate being controlled.

I did. Maybe I still do. But that's separate from my other feelings.

For Shane.

Libby said that she didn't want to talk about Shane. She said that Guido had offered his place in the Alps if she wanted to come visit.

But you said no?

I almost went. But by that time, I was intrigued by Shane, and the group here. Were you hiding this friend, Baptiste? How come I never met him?

You're funny.

You liked him.

Why do you say that?

I'm not stupid. You hid him because you liked him. Isn't that right?

Oh, Libby. You don't know everything.

You're right. I only know what you tell me. Wasn't that your famous line? You always used that on us kids when you were jonesing for information and secrets. I guess we all have secrets, Mom. You probably thought that I would judge you. Didn't you?

Lucille was quiet.

I think it's wonderful to have love, Libby said. I would have been happy for you. I'm not as moral as you think. And I see you. I see that you are lonely. And if you had decided to show us this French man, we all would have been pleased. I'm not as selfish as I used to be.

It was nothing, Libby. And it's past.

Libby snapped off her gloves and announced that she was done. Perfect for this Baptiste.

They crossed back over to Phuket in the early morning on a larger boat, one with life jackets and two decks. Everyone took shelter in the lower deck because the sea was rough, and within two hours, most of the passengers were throwing up into buckets, or onto the floor, or over the gunnels. Lucille hadn't eaten any breakfast that morning, and though she felt queasy, she had nothing in her stomach to get rid of. Libby slept as if a mere child, a baby, her head against Lucille's shoulder.

They took an afternoon flight to Bangkok. Lucille had asked Libby to stay with her for one night, before Lucille's morning flight to Paris, but Libby said no. She wanted to go back. She was very certain. She hugged Lucille at the arrival doors. She was wearing her backpack and Lucille didn't know where to put her arms, for she couldn't wrap them around the extra burden, and so she ended up with her hands on Libby's hips, which felt cold and wrong. She touched Libby's face with one palm and said, I love you. Take a cab, Lucille said, I'll pay.

Libby shook her head. She lifted a hand for a motorcycle taxi, and then clambered on behind the driver, slipped into a helmet, put her arms around the driver's waist, chest pressed hard against the driver's back, and she was gone into the chaos of the Bangkok night.

Lucille had planned on giving Libby some extra money, a few thousand baht and several hundred dollars, just to carry her through for the next while, but in the commotion of arriving and departing, she had forgotten. And Libby hadn't asked. And now she was gone.

Lucille took a room at a hotel near the airport. She bathed. She plucked. She scraped at the heels of her feet with an emery board. She cleaned her nails and applied new polish. Fingernails and toenails. She checked her email from work, found that the world had carried on without her, and closed it without reading anything. Then she opened her private email, and she wrote a note to Morris.

∾

Morris,

I just watched our daughter tear off on the back of a motorcycle into the melee of a city that runs on bedlam. On my way south by bus last week I saw a motorcyclist get hit and fall to the pavement. Certainly dead. And the traffic did not stop! People deliberately drive their cars around the victim, barely avoiding the poor man, and when the police finally appear, they run out into the street and blow ferociously on their whistles and wave their arms and then drag the body off to the side of the road. The priority here appears to be keeping the traffic moving, regardless of corpses on the road. And so, there was Libby rushing off on a motorcycle into the night. With a complete stranger. Until I hear differently, I will assume she is alive. She is going back to Pattaya to be with Shane, her boyfriend slash cult leader. How crazy does that sound? I managed to pull her away for a week and we spent our time on an island in the gulf, but I failed to convince her of anything important. She is stubborn still, like you. And full of strange passions, like you. And illogical, like you. And so it is, out of great despair and hope, that I turn to you. I know that you have a baby. I know that life is full. But might you take time to write Libby? And appeal to her?

Be kind. Be careful. If you were to meet this Shane you would throttle him. Who has a name like that? I hear it and I think of chain and shame and pain. Oh, Morris. The man feeds his followers (all women) little drops of candy laced with poison. Drops these candies down on the path that his women then follow. He leads them into ways of unrighteousness. He speaks with a little bit of a lisp, and he folds his hands in his dangerous lap — and the word is apt for he is surrounded by lapdogs, of which Libby appears to be one — and he talks nonsense out of both sides of his mouth. Sometimes I heard my own voice in his, and I wondered if I did the same. If we all do the same. Pretend at wisdom when it is only folly and madness. Why this need to be right? Why this desire to sway? What little fissures have we produced in our beautiful Libby that would allow her to choose that man? Where did we go wrong? What damage did we do? Why didn't we stay together? Why didn't we love each other more? Of course, there are no good answers. And even the questions are full of regret and unhappiness. She told me that I was lonely. Am I? Do I exude remoteness? Sadness? As soon as I showed up at that place, and as soon as I saw her walking towards me in her ugly jean dress, her uniform, I knew that I had chosen poorly. I shouldn't have gone to her. I should have turned and run. I should have left her to her own subterfuge. I didn't recognize her. Though there were moments, when she spoke, that I saw briefly the glimmers of the Libby we knew. Scepticism, irony, self-awareness. And then it flew away.

Please write to her. Use trickery, fine words, compassion, anything. I fear it won't help, but at least it will be an attempt. She loves you, confesses everything to you, which in the past has led to difficulties, but here, now, she needs you. I need you. Can you do that?

Lucille

She flew Qatar Airways to Paris. She was stuck in the last seat, at the back of the plane, right next to the washrooms. A constant parade of humanity passing by to void themselves. She slept. Ate a little from the meals offered. Slept some more. The hostesses were all tall and young and they wore matching red hats pinned to their dark hair. She woke one time and saw Libby's face approaching, but it was only a hostess, who had Libby's eyes. She had not sent the email to Morris. Upon rereading it, before clicking Send, she had realized that the writing of the letter had been enough, and she had realized that it was not true that she needed Morris, and she had realized that her voice was too whiny, too strident, and that her words were desperate. Libby would choose. And Lucille would go on being Lucille, living out her small life in a small city in the middle of the continent. And so, she had trashed the note and closed her phone.

She watched a movie on the little screen before her. A film called *Sils Maria*, or something like that. She was not good with titles. She watched it. Was pleased to have discovered it. Was excited by the relationship between an older woman and a younger woman. Thought that young women today were more powerful and yet less aware of their complex edges than she had been at that age. Sex was not simple. Or the motives behind sex. The intentions behind the motives behind sex. All motives. All intentions. All wishes. None of this was simple. Her father had received letters once a month from Eva, the German. For two years after climbing Kilimanjaro. Lucille had found and read them. They were Eva's words, she never saw her father's words, but Eva's were special words, provocative words. She picked up the pages, put them down, and found them again a week later and read them entirely, because she could not stop herself. And watched her father now, differently. And her mother. And was caught one day by her father, in his study — she was sitting on his chair, her feet tucked up, holding one of the letters. The rage, the hissing, the pledge to silence, your mother cannot know, it is over in any case, but your mother cannot know, and how stupid of Lucille to agree that her mother could not know, but what else could she do, and then the silence, and the gratuitous favours, and the distrust.

Lucille drove a tow truck that summer, her father's idea, as if he wanted her to grow up. And so, she worked for a friend of her father's, at a dealership, picking up used cars, pulling them back to the car lot, dropping them off at the mechanics' bay, wearing shorts, a halter top, the mechanics flirting with her, not she with them, hating the talk, the jokes, turning away as if she didn't hear, knowing that she could have them fired just like that if she mentioned their words to the boss, but not talking about it, because she didn't want to embarrass herself. And then away, leaving home, moving into an apartment on Langside, going to university. Leaving her poor mother, who didn't even know how a bank account worked, or where money came from, or that she should store money away for a rainy day. For if there was one solid fact in the world, besides death, it was that rainy days would come. When the money saved in secret would be absolutely required. Her mother had not believed that poverty was possible. Could not fathom it. What Lucille had learned from observing the mistakes of her mother was that preparation was everything. Control. Regulation. Discipline.

And then came Morris, seducing her in a sideways manner, with ideas, and words, not vulgar words, but words about the ideas, the central idea being to draw her towards him. She was twenty-four, in school still, going to therapy, pushing Morris away like a Victorian. No sex till marriage. She was unwavering. He acquiesced, poor man. To want was lovely. To want to the extreme was brilliant. Abstention in all matters. Feeling. Hunger. Desire. But no abstention of the mind. This was when she took up smoking. Which would kill her but hadn't yet. Yet, knives could kill as well. And pills. And despair. And leaps from tall buildings. And fire. And pestilence. And snakebite. And guns. Martin knew about guns. Knew they were dangerous. But didn't know that he would be killed by friendly fire. Two simple and contradictory words. She had not truly understood that term until she heard it out of the mouth of Morris, who had used it so effortlessly when announcing Martin's death. What is that? she asked. What does that mean? Is it a joke? She had never been good with jokes. She was not a simpleton. She preferred subtlety, inference, the hint of humour, perhaps even not-humour, but close to humour. A wry tongue. It wasn't that she hadn't had sex before, she had, with several men, but Morris was different, though he didn't want to be different, he wanted her. She said that he might touch her, and play with her, but he couldn't penetrate her. Play with her! As if she were a doll. And so, he penetrated her with his thoughts, and his words, and now she missed him, at this moment, and thought it a humorous tragedy that he had managed to get himself snipped and then put back together in order to seed young Jill. To be old was to be fallow. For a woman. And she was old. And fallow. No more seeding. *There was an old woman, I have heard tell, She went to market, Her eggs to sell.* The island bungalow where she stayed with Libby had not had a mirror, and so for a week they had used each other to see if everything was in order. Teeth clean. Hair in place. Dress right. Buttons correct. It had turned into little moments of caretaking, reaching out to touch each other, to straighten themselves out, to see oneself only through the eyes of the other. And so, when Lucille had finally seen herself in the brilliantly lit bathroom mirror of her airport hotel room, she had been horrified. She was old. How careless of her. Of Libby. And yet, Libby had never said this to her. She had only said, upon straightening her top, or touching her hair, You look beautiful, Mama. And touched Lucille's nose with her own, an act of comfort that Lucille had used when Libby was young and anxious and had not wanted to go to school or go to a friend's house for a sleepover — touch noses and stare into each other's eyes and say, It will be fine. All is fine. Should she have rubbed noses with Libby at the airport before she climbed onto the back of the motorcycle? Would it have been allowed? What was allowed anymore?

Her prime worry in life was being caught. Caught smoking. Caught naked. Caught hiding. Caught in anger. Misspelling a word. Quoting Freud. Whom she admired. For his artful writing, his contradictions, the libido, the death drive. But Freud was all wrong these days. Out of favour. No more flavour in Freud! Exclamation mark! She hated exclamation marks. And adverbs. She hated them terribly! Safer to quote Jung, who said that children are unconsciously driven in a direction that is intended to compensate for everything that was left unfulfilled in the lives of their parents. What was safe in knowing that?

DAVID BERGEN

When she was in her early forties, Lucille attended a two-week conference on attachment in Modena, Italy. The sessions were held in a former convent, below the village. In the evenings, the participants would leave the convent and walk up the mountain to the village to eat dinner. Seven courses, ending with chocolate shot glasses that held various liqueurs. Lucille found herself, every evening, seated beside Mohammed, a psychoanalyst from Paris, who was her age, and who she found was a fine conversationalist. They spoke of travelling. They spoke of books they had read. He asked her many questions about herself, and he paid attention to her answers. They usually walked back down the mountain together late at night, sometimes taking detours through the smaller lanes, and in the end, they found themselves alone, for the larger group had gone ahead. She felt flattered by the attention Mohammed gave her. They were both playing at something, but because he had a wife and three children back in Paris, and she was married with her own three children, it didn't appear that much harm could be done in spending the warm evenings at supper together and then wandering around the village and eventually descending to the convent, where the men were lodged in a separate building from the women. It all felt safe. In fact, when Lucille considered the possibility of any sort of romance, she found it laughable, for she and Mohammed were literally locked into their separate buildings. A guardian bolted the gates at midnight, and this eliminated any movement between the two buildings. She felt safe. She imagined that this was how nuns must feel.

One evening after dinner, walking down the mountain together, past little shops where young men stood in groups and studied the two of them as they passed, sometimes whistling and calling out to Lucille, Mohammed took her hand when she stumbled on the cobblestones, and even when she had regained her balance, he did not let her go. She was okay with this. She found it to be quite innocent. Perhaps she saw herself as a nun.

At the gate to his compound, he asked her to join him. In his room.

She laughed and said that she couldn't. It would be too strange to enter his room, which was meant for men, and what would happen if she was caught?

He said that he would make sure she wasn't caught.

Not tonight, she said. He said okay and kissed her on the cheek.

He asked her every night after that, and every night, she said no.

On the second-last day of the conference, he asked if she didn't want to walk up to the village with him. He wanted to get souvenirs for his children. She agreed. She would look for souvenirs for her children as well, though she had no desire. She was not the kind of woman who came home from trips bearing gifts.

He bought a watercolour set for each of his children, and he bought a necklace for his wife. He asked Lucille to try it on. Just to see.

She was uncomfortable with this, but she acquiesced. He said that it was perfect. He asked if she was going to get something for her husband.

She said that her husband had everything he needed. In any case, her suitcase was small, and she had no room for extra things.

That night, they again ate at the same table. Seated beside each other. As usual, there were others at the table, laughing and drinking and talking, and Lucille saw that many of them had become good friends, for there was a conviviality in the conversation that was very natural. She had been so focused on Mohammed that she had perhaps missed out on making new friends, on exploring new ideas. She was a little bit sorry, but not too much.

That night, as they reached their lodgings, Mohammed said that he would really like her to come to his room. It was private. No one would know. He said that he would like to make love to her. I think you feel the same, he said.

She was quiet, and he took that silence for either agreement or the proximity of agreement. He kissed her. She let him.

Come, he said, and he took her hand.

She pulled away. She said that when he had bought the necklace for his wife, and when she had helped him by trying it on, she had only then realized that his wife was in Paris. That his wife was taking care of the children while he was here, with her. That his wife must be very important to him. He was still with her, wasn't he? He bought her gifts. That was a wonderful thing. She said that she would go to her own room now, and he would go to his.

Mohammed became agitated. He said that what happened here, on this mountain, in this nunnery—he said the word *nunnery* with some contempt—was completely removed from the world he lived in with his family. Sometimes sex is just sex, he said. He said that he hated being bald. He wanted a full head of hair.

And then what? she asked. You'd be a different man? A happier man? A sexier man? You'd lose your old self? And have a new you? Hair is everything?

She squeezed his hand and left him standing there.

∞

On the TGV from Paris to Montpellier, her purse was stolen. In it was her passport, and her makeup, and her notebook, and her wallet, and her phone, and her driver's licence, and her extra credit card, and her ATM card, and her cash, and her lip balm, and her reading glasses. Other things as well, which she would register the loss of over the next few days, such as the little tin of Motrin from which she would take one pill whenever she anticipated walking long distances.

She had had a brief conversation on the train half an hour out of Paris with a woman who had been standing in the aisle. The woman claimed that Lucille was in her seat. Perhaps Lucille had misread her ticket? They'd compared tickets. It turned out that the woman was in the wrong car. The woman apologized profusely. It was her fault. So sorry. She was wearing a red jacket, dark glasses, and she was maybe forty or forty-five years old. She spoke French with an accent. Though Lucille couldn't have said what kind of accent. Eastern European? The woman in the red jacket had asked where Lucille was from. She loved Canada, she said. I love your President. And then she had apologized one last time and moved up the aisle and disappeared through the doors, which sucked shut behind her. Lucille had turned to the window to watch the landscape flash by, though there was not much to see. Embankments. Cement.

The occasional road. Cars and trucks on the freeway. She had hoped to see farms, cows, barns. But when that did happen, she saw them for a second and then they were gone.

There had been a feeling, while talking to the woman, of something behind her, and when she'd turned to look, she saw nothing, though she smelled something, a scent of body odour, which left her feeling uneasy, but then she turned back to the woman, who was still apologizing.

It had been half an hour or so after talking to the woman in the red jacket that she discovered her purse was missing. She did not panic at first. She did not think of the red blazer, or the woman. The purse might have slipped between the seats. Or she'd left it in her suitcase, which seemed unlikely, but possible. She was sometimes absent-minded. She retrieved her suitcase from the overhead compartment, set it on the seat, and rummaged through her clothes. No purse. She closed the suitcase and put it back in the overhead bin. She bent forward to look under the seats. There was a man seated directly behind her. He was sleeping, a book in his lap. She asked the young woman in the seat in front of her if she had seen a purse, black leather, with a shoulder strap. The woman shook her head.

Lucille said that her purse had been stolen.

The woman made a face of pity, or perhaps it was one of annoyance. In any case, the woman said that it happened often. These people came on the train and pretended to have your seat, and they distracted you, and then took your possessions. She said the word *possessions* with great emphasis.

Lucille said it wasn't her possessions that concerned her. It was her identification. Her phone. Her passport.

The woman said that of course they would want the passport first and foremost.

Something about the woman, perhaps her age, reminded Lucille of the woman in the red jacket, and the confusion around the tickets and the seating, and she realized what had happened.

The woman said that Lucille should speak to the concierge.

The concierge repeated what the woman had said, that the thieves distracted you. They worked in teams. He said that she would have to make a report with the police in Montpellier.

Lucille described the woman. She used her hands, she spoke slowly, she dug for the details and the right words.

The concierge made a gesture and he said that the thieves would be gone by now. Or they would have changed clothes. They had disguises. He was sorry for her loss.

The phrase was extreme. No one had died. She realized that the language barrier might have made his words bigger, more extravagant. She asked him if the *gare de police* in Montpellier was close to the central *gare de train*. He didn't understand at first, and so she kept offering variations of the word *gare*, until finally he smiled and said that the *commissariat de police* was not far from the *gare*. He told her the street. He indicated right and then left and then right and he talked about a police hotel. Thirteen minutes, *à pied*.

She asked him if he didn't want to warn others on the train.

We can do nothing, Madame. He repeated the word *nothing*. He said that a warning would just elevate the anxiety. And for what? *Désolé*. He seemed absolutely indifferent.

She thanked him.

He said that it was nothing. And then, as if the idea had just entered his head, or perhaps he now pitied her, he said that she should check the garbage disposals on the train. Sometimes the thieves simply wanted the cash and they took this and threw the purse or the sack into the garbage. He said that she might want to check. And he left her standing there.

And so, taking his advice, she walked through the various cars, pushing her arm deep into each of the garbage bins that she found in the bathrooms and at the end of each of the cars. She found paper bags, and wrappers from candy, and used Kleenex, and by the time she had covered the length of the train, all she had for her efforts was dirty hands. No purse.

She returned to her seat and sat. She was surprised at how calm she felt.

She dragged her suitcase behind her in the heat of the city. She might have hailed a taxi, but she had no money. And so, she walked, passing building upon building, all very grey and all very ugly. When she finally stumbled upon the *commissariat*, she was sweating and tired and near tears. She told the man in uniform at the front desk that she wanted to report a theft.

He made a phone call and told her to sit. She sat for a long time. It was cool in the building and she watched the people pass in and out of the doorways. Everyone walked quickly, with great purpose, some in uniform, some not. Even those not in official uniform had uniforms of a sort, the men in suits and black shoes, the women in blouses and jackets and thin skirts and low shoes. Everyone was thin, the women especially, or so it seemed.

A woman in a police uniform appeared and listened to her story. She asked Lucille if she had been hurt. Was there violence?

No, no violence, Lucille said. I am not hurt. Other than my pride. My passport was taken. My identification. My cash. My credit cards. Everything.

The woman asked if she had made a statement to the rail company.

They sent me here. They said I must report the theft here.

First, it is necessary to report to the rail company, fill out the proper forms, and then report to us. Then we oversee those forms and we will take your statement. The woman finished talking, lifted a hand to her mouth, and yawned.

What will you do once I've told you my story and all these forms have been filled out? Lucille asked. What recourse do I have? Will I find my passport? My purse? Will someone hunt down the culprits? Lucille already knew the answers to her questions, but she felt compelled to ask them.

The woman said that not much else could be done. This was a common occurrence. What was necessary was the proper forms.

To what end? Lucille asked. For what reason?

The woman said, For the reason of order. And organization. It is impossible to begin to look for the thieves until we have a description of the thieves. You cannot catch something that you know nothing about.

I lost my phone as well, Lucille said. Could I use a phone here? To make a call to the embassy?

What country are you from?

Lucille told her and the woman sighed and then gestured for Lucille to follow her. And so, she did, wheeling her suitcase across the marble floor. They ascended via an elevator that had two sets of doors, one accordion-like, one solid, and it was the accordion doors that the woman pulled shut first. And then the solid doors shut on their own. The ride to the third floor was a quiet one.

They exited into a corridor with many doors. The woman led Lucille to one of the doors, opened it, and asked her to please step in. There was a desk and two chairs. A stand-up fan was on high speed. A telephone.

The woman pointed to the phone.

Lucille said that she didn't know the number of the embassy, and she couldn't look for it, as she didn't have her phone.

The woman shrugged and left the room.

Lucille sat and waited. She picked up the phone and listened to the dial tone. She set it down. She had a phone number. Baptiste had written it down in his note to her. It was for his sister's house, where he was staying temporarily. Should you need it, he wrote. But she was aghast to think of calling, like a teenager, to ask for help.

The door finally opened, and a man entered. He held a sheaf of papers. He wore a white shirt, and a black tie that was loose at the collar. He sat down across from Lucille. He introduced himself as Inspecteur Bidoux.

There was a robber, he announced.

Yes.

On the train.

Yes, on the train, Lucille said. At least, I believe so. That's where I noticed that my purse was gone. And everything with it.

You are not sure.

I am sure. It was on the train.

The inspector took a pen from his pocket and arranged the papers on the desk and asked her name.

Lucille gave it. And then she gave her nationality, and her date of birth, and her marriage status, and how many children she had, and her address in Canada, and her occupation—when she told him, he raised an eyebrow. He said that he and his wife had seen someone like her a year ago. About the marriage. He made a wry face. He said that after much talking, and much discussion, and some fighting, they were now divorced. So. As if to say, What use was she? Lucille said that she was sorry. He said that there was no need to be sorry. He was a happier man now. And his wife was happier. The children, well, they were not so happy. He said that he had been accused of overwhelming his young daughter, and of pouring too much of his thoughts into her. Of giving her too much information. She was ten years old. He saw now that he had not done her any good by confessing to her what she had no right to know. He said that he hoped his daughter would survive.

Lucille said that children were surprisingly resilient.

Do you think so? the inspector asked.

Lucille said yes, though she had no idea what the daughter was truly like.

The inspector picked up his pen once again and Lucille gave the reason for her visit, and how long she would be staying, and where she would be staying. Uzès. He asked the name of the family with whom she would be staying. She didn't know. She had never paid attention to Baptiste's family name. Renard, she said. Or Renaud. One or the other.

It can't be one or the other, the inspector said. It can only be one. Which one?

Lucille excused herself and asked if she might look in her suitcase. She pointed at her baggage beside her.

It is safe? the inspector asked.

Is what safe?

The valise.

Of course, it's safe.

Well then, please, he said, and he gestured at her bag.

She found the invitation to Baptiste's wedding stuck in a side pouch of the suitcase. She read the invitation and said that the family name was Renard. The inspector wrote it down. He asked if the family Renard knew the time of her arrival.

It was a strange question. She said that she planned to travel up to Uzès on Friday. Today was Wednesday. The wedding was Sunday. She didn't know if they knew her exact arrival time.

He asked how she would get to Uzès.

She was going to hire a car.

Rent?

Yes.

He said that this was impossible now without a driver's licence. Or a passport. Or money.

Lucille knew all of this, of course, but she hadn't wanted to appear weak, or in need. She said that she would find a way.

He suggested that she might fly, and he flapped his arms.

She imagined him with his ten-year-old daughter.

He asked if she knew someone in Montpellier. Someone who might give her assistance.

Only the Renard family, she said. But I don't *know* them.

You are going to the wedding?

Yes, but.

And so, you know someone. Unless you are sabotaging the wedding? He smiled.

She said that it was an old friend, from a while back. She had been invited, and now she was here, by chance.

He said that she of all people should know that nothing happened by chance. Especially a trip from Canada to France for a wedding.

For some reason, perhaps because he had flapped his arms loosely, and he seemed loose in general, she told him that she had just come from Thailand, where she had visited her daughter, who was also getting married. Why she said what was not yet true, she did not know. Though it felt true, and even as she spilled out this little confession, she realized that Libby might do exactly that, and forever after suffer the consequences. But we all suffer the consequences of our decisions, our actions. It was just that some consequences were more ominous.

So many marriages, he said, and he clapped his hands. Congratulations. He asked if her daughter was already married.

Lucille shook her head and said that her daughter might be planning a wedding. This was the frightening part.

And you would go back there, for the marriage?

No.

He was surprised. But it is your daughter.

She said that she had great doubts about marriage in general. He nodded in agreement. She, too, was now being loose. She saw herself as if from above — an older woman, hair pestered by the fan, seated on the edge of her chair, knees together, hands in her lap, sharing thoughts that were not in fact true. Perhaps it was the heat. Perhaps it was the loss of her identity. She felt a flutter of desire. It was between her legs, almost shocking, uncalled for, but then, desire is never beckoned. She wondered if this feeling, both embarrassing and welcoming, was because of her newly achieved anonymity, which she knew might bring on all sorts of idiosyncratic traits. Such as sexual laxness. She didn't find the inspector particularly attractive. And so, what was it? She closed her eyes briefly and breathed slowly. When she opened her eyes again, he was watching her. His own eyes were dark brown. He was swarthy. He could have been the brother or cousin of Mohammed, her non-lover from those two weeks in Italy, who was also French. The darkish growth at the jaw. The fruitful mouth. Substantial. She wanted to touch his hand on the table. The black hair on his knuckles. If he asked to kiss her, or just kissed her, she would not push him away. She leaned in. Her body trembled and she was faint.

He asked if she would like some water.

She said, Yes, please.

He stood and left and returned a few minutes later with two glasses of water and set one down before her. The glass had fingerprints on it, and it was dirty, but she picked it up and drank. She wondered if it was possible to get sick in the south of France from drinking water in this manner. Hepatitis. Cholera. How absurd. She had never considered this in Southeast Asia, and now, here she was in one of the most civilized countries in the world, worrying about disease when it was her own dis-ease she should be concerned about. Her light-headedness, her lack of boundaries in this conversation, her desire, the unexpected pleasure of anonymity.

The inspector said that the city of Montpellier did not have a Canadian embassy. That was in Paris. There was a Canadian consulate in Toulouse, and one in Lyons. The one in Lyons was closer to Uzès, and so she might want to go there. He said that she would have to go in person and present herself at the consulate. They would let her in because she was a citizen of the country. They would not let him in. But they would allow her entry, and it would be there that she would receive a temporary passport. The problem, he said, was that it would take a few days. And over the weekend, it would be difficult. He suggested that she go to the wedding in Uzès first, enjoy herself, and then travel to Lyons. Three hours maximum by car. If she had a car.

She didn't, but she would find a way.

He said that of course she would find a way. Her French was very passable. And she was contained. And she was capable.

She felt like crying, and she wondered if it was the comment on her French or her being capable. Maybe both. Perhaps what he had truly meant to say was that she spoke a contained French. Which she would have accepted as a compliment and high praise. Containment was good.

Who will you call? the inspector asked.

She said that she would call the house of Renard.

The inspector gestured at the phone and said that he would be present during the call.

You don't trust me? Lucille asked.

Of course. But this is a police station. And that is not a public phone. You might be calling all over the world.

Why would I do that?

People can be crazy.

I'm not crazy.

I can see that.

You didn't ask for a description of the woman on the train. The one who took my purse.

He shook his head. He said that the woman was known. She was familiar. She had many different looks. Different hair. Different accents. Did she ask you what country you were from?

Yes.

And did she say that she loved your Prime Minister?

She said President. I didn't correct her. Lucille paused. And said, I should have known right then. Yes?

The inspector smiled ruefully. He said that one day these people would be caught. But right now, Lucille would make contact with the family Renard. Please.

There were stars glowing above her and she heard the sound of a car in the street below and then voices and then it was quiet again and she got out of bed and stepped out onto the terrace that was attached to the bedroom and she stood in the heat of the night and looked up at the real sky now, but it was cloudy and there was no sky to be seen. She had been given Céline's room. Baptiste's niece, the daughter of Colette and André. Lucille had protested and said that an air mattress or a blanket on the couch would be adequate, but Colette had insisted. And so, she found herself in a child's room surrounded by dolls and stuffed animals and glow-in-the-dark stars on the ceiling, sleeping in a bed that was too short for her.

They had eaten, Colette and André and she, beneath the arbour on the patio. A late dinner of lamb and potatoes with rosemary, and a salad prepared by André, and they had finished two bottles of wine from the Languedoc region, described lovingly by Colette, who reminded Lucille of Baptiste. The same shape of eyes, the same inflections in the voice, the same knowledge of wine. Colette was kinder than André, who seemed distant, perhaps put upon. Of course. Lucille would feel the same. A strange woman shows up empty-handed and bereft, begging for a room. It was indefensible.

It was only later in the evening, after a glass of Chartreuse, that André had warmed to her. The conversation had turned to his hobbies, of which he had one, cycling, and when Lucille said that she cycled as well, which was true, though certainly not as seriously as André, he opened up. She had ridden the Rockies, she said. A three-day trip of four hundred kilometres. A large group, she told him, well supported. Her main problem was a fear of logging trucks, or big trucks in general, for what happened was that the truck swept by, and all seemed fine, and then the backdraft came along and pulled you towards the rear wheels and of course it felt like you might be devoured by those wheels. She paused. Drank a little more. Felt heady. He asked about her bike, but she could not give him great details. She knew the name, but that was all. She rode for pleasure. Not for knowledge. He described his own bike, and said that in the morning, early, he would be going out. He liked to ride before heading into surgery. He did three stapedectomies a day, in the morning, and in the afternoon, he was in the clinic. Lucille said that her ex-husband had had stapedectomies in both ears, at different times, of course, and she had been amazed at the benefit. Though she was no longer living with him, and so he didn't have to listen to her anymore. He was listening to someone else now.

It was that glass of Chartreuse that had relaxed her tongue. André had poured her a small glass, and it shimmered green as he lovingly described it as a French liqueur made by the Carthusian monks since 1737. The initial taste was sweet, but the aftertaste was vegetal. She should be careful, but then, she didn't really care. Colette laughed when Lucille talked about her ex-husband listening to someone else. She touched Lucille's arm.

Earlier, before dinner, in her room, she had found one of her credit cards in her jeans pocket, and she had been so amazed and relieved that she had sat holding the card for a long time, turning it over, not believing her good fortune. At the same time, she had been surprised that this little plastic rectangle could mean so much. She considered announcing to her hosts that she would now be able to take a hotel room, and they could have the house to themselves, but that might be rude, and so she slipped the card back into her pocket. She felt more independent now, and with the independence came confidence. She could choose her life again. In any case, she made a few phone calls using Colette's phone and she cancelled her remaining cards, and she called the consulate in Lyons regarding an application for a temporary passport, and when she learned that the consulate was closed for renovations, she called Toulouse and spoke to someone there. She was given instructions, she was asked if she had a police report. She did. After the call, she thought of the various cogs in the grand machinery of bureaucracy that existed for people such as her. She was grateful. Colette had given her a laptop to use, and she had logged in to her Gmail and sent Morris a note saying that she would be out of contact for the next week. She was in France. She had been robbed of everything. She was fine. She was going to a wedding. She said that she had a piece of paper in her pocket, on which she had written, My Name is Lucille Black, and so she now had some way of knowing who she was. Ha!

She did not ask Morris about Libby. Ever since she had lost her phone, she had not given her much thought. She did not miss the ping of a text coming in. She did not miss scrolling and looking and scrolling and wondering. She felt light-headed, which is how she often felt when on the edge of a precipice, or when she stood looking down from a great height. An urge to jump. Or she imagined herself jumping. Or falling. And with that came a sense of weightlessness.

And she felt an even greater sense of weightlessness later that evening, just after the liqueur was poured, when Colette leaned forward and placed her elbows on the table and rested her narrow chin on her hands and said that she would now tell Lucille what she wasn't able to say earlier with Céline present. She said that Inèz had gotten, how do you call it, cold feet, and she had stopped the wedding. Just the day before. With the tents raised at the farm, and the caterers ready, and the flowers ordered, it was finished. She said that Baptiste was up at the house in Uzès, alone, and he had called to give her the news. He was quite calm. Surprisingly so. And this was wrong. She said that she was worried, for Baptiste was a bit like their mother had been, melancholic, and she worried that he would do something harmful. She had talked to him on the phone earlier, before dinner, and he had just gone for a swim, and he was about to cook something, and she asked him if she should come there, to be with him, but he said that he was fine. He asked if she could let people know. The guests. And she agreed. She would do that in the morning. It was very difficult. She said that he was embarrassed, and she told him that it was Inèz who should be ashamed. But overall, wasn't this better? To have not suffered the uncertainty later? To have not entered a marriage that was doomed in any case? She said all the wrong things, of course. She should have been kinder, more sympathetic. But she was happy inside, secretly, for she had distrusted Inèz from the get-go. It wasn't a good match. She said that Baptiste had been too desperate for love. Too hasty. It was all too cruel. She said that women these days were in the midst of some sort of grand freedom, perhaps they had been trapped and held hostage for too long, but now they were finding freedom, and they were discovering choice, and it was a man like her brother who would suffer from that freedom. This was very old-fashioned thinking, she said, but this was how she felt. Poor him.

Lucille said that she was so sorry. And she uttered a single word, Oh, and it sounded too sad, but she didn't know how to take it back.

Colette said that her main worry, and this was just a sister being a sister of a brother who didn't have a mother to fret over him, was that there would have been no children, of course, for Inèz was older, no one knew her age, for she hadn't divulged that, but she looked younger than she was, perhaps even tried too hard, but the truth of the matter was she was beyond child-bearing years, and had adult children of her own, and Colette had worried about this, for Baptiste loved children, he adored his niece, and she had worried that one day he would regret the loss, the lack.

They had been speaking English, though André and Colette sometimes broke into French with each other, but for most of the evening the conversation was in English, and so Lucille heard very clearly the description of Inèz, and she heard André say, She is a bitch.

That was when Lucille excused herself and went to the bathroom and washed her hands, and saw herself in the mirror, and wondered at the melancholic pleasure that she had felt upon hearing André's assessment. When she returned, Colette was alone at the table. There were animal sounds in the shrubbery. The fairy lights in the trees cast a soft light onto the table. The candles were still burning. Colette was smoking. She said that her husband hated it when she smoked, but now that he was off to bed, she was free to do as she pleased. Would Lucille like one? Yes, Lucille said. Colette asked if she would like another drop of Chartreuse. Yes, please. Colette apologized for her husband's language earlier. He tended to get upset because he was very protective of Baptiste. But his words were not necessary. She said that Inèz was lovely. She was perhaps smarter than everyone believed her to be. She must have seen something in the relationship that frightened her. Or warned her. Baptiste could be very strong-willed. And demanding. And he was anxious to have this wedding. This party. Colette said that she was sorry for Baptiste but she was also not sorry. He lived in a state of unconsciousness. Perhaps this was just men in general. She said that she often thought that her own husband was only partially conscious of his relationship with her. Sometimes it seemed he loved his bicycle more than her. Or his work. Or his car. And that made it difficult. She said that a man's instincts were different from a woman's, though both had a biological instinct, the preservation of the species. Still, women were overtaken by children, and men by their exterior creations. She said that this was why men ran away to another woman, or back to their mother, or knocked their heads against the walls of success, or built rockets and flew to the moon. They appeared to believe that they were choosing, when in fact they were simply following the scent of something, which might resemble the sweetness of success, and often turned into the sour smell of failure.

She said that, as a child, some of her favourite stories had been those of King Arthur, in particular Sir Gawain, where the central riddle had been, what does a woman truly want? And the ultimate answer was that a woman wants to be able to choose. Even an older woman like Inèz, who could no longer bear children and had lived past her usefulness, and because of this, she created chaos and ended up, ultimately, being ugly. In everyone's eyes, save for Baptiste's.

She said that Baptiste appeared to want to test the notions of chivalry. He would accept his ugly lady, and he would tame chaos. He would act in public the same way he would act in private. Only, his ugly lady would not turn into a beautiful young woman. And his woman would choose not to be with him.

But she chose, Lucille said. And it is useless to argue with someone who chooses. To be a judge of that choice.

Colette shrugged. She said, It is one thing to choose, and it is another to keep changing your mind. That is ambivalence. And ambivalence in marriage, and in love, is cruel. If Inèz were sitting here, right now, with us, I would not hesitate to use my husband's word. What makes her think that she is better than us? Baptiste is lucky. How do you say? *Échapper belle?* And even though I am happy that Baptiste will not have to suffer her arrogance, I feel for him. He is unfortunate with love.

She said that, in the morning, she would tell Baptiste that Lucille had arrived. And that she was staying with them. She said that Baptiste had no intention of coming back here for some time. Not until *la poussière* had settled. Her brother felt shame, which was unnecessary but predictable. She planned on driving up there tomorrow. She didn't like him being there alone. Would Lucille join her?

Lucille said that she wasn't sure. What good could she do? She was just a distant friend.

Colette said that it would be one more disappointment for Baptiste if Lucille didn't come. He had spoken of her so fondly. Perhaps even loved her in some way. And now he was alone again. He had suffered the most when their mother died. The son and the mother, Colette said. Hey? Very close. She said, My sister and I, not so close to her. There is something between mothers and daughters, don't you think? Some competition. Sharp edges. A smothering.

She asked if Lucille had daughters.

Two.

Then you understand.

Lucille said that the mother was perhaps too close to the action and too close to the smothering to understand the danger. The daughter felt the danger and responded. Through rejection. Anger. Disdain. Which led to guilt, and grudging acts of kindness.

Colette laughed. She lit another cigarette. Yes. Exactly. Still, she missed her mother dearly. She had been brilliant. A master of creation. Though her mother had a hard time accepting her own brilliance. She fluctuated between self-abnegation and great ego. Like Baptiste.

You must join me tomorrow, Colette said. Céline will stay here with her father.

Lucille was quiet. The crickets called. The candles flickered. One went out. She said that she was sorry, but she would not come. She knew that Baptiste would want to see her, and she might even be a distraction for him at this time, but she didn't think a distraction was a good enough reason to go. She was to leave the following week for home, and she needed a passport, and she didn't know how long that would take. She paused. I hope you understand. I hope that Baptiste understands.

Of course. I will tell him.

Colette put out her cigarette and stood. Began to gather the dishes. Lucille stood as well and picked up a few glasses.

Colette said that it was not necessary. Please. It was late. The cleanup would happen in the morning. Good night.

Lucille said good night and found her way back to her room. She heard voices later, Colette's and André's, Colette's voice strident. They might be talking about her, about her ingratitude. An old woman who lacked grace. Or perhaps they were fighting about Colette's smoking. Or sex. Or André's preference for bicycles. Anything was possible.

And now, at 3 a.m., standing on the little balcony, the house was quiet. The family was sleeping. She was not. She had not told the whole truth earlier when she gave her reasons for not going to Uzès. She couldn't have told the whole truth. Which was that she was tired of others. Of being wanted. Of the oppression of others' needs. Of the panic she had felt when she thought of driving up to the house in Uzès. Of seeing Baptiste. Of duty. Of expectations. She saw now that she had used the wedding as an excuse to run from her dire life. And here she was, still in dire circumstances. Laughable, really. What did she want? She wanted to sit on a train by herself, and order an espresso, and fondle her single credit card, and watch the berms rush by, and talk to no one, and anticipate Mozart's Requiem, which was to be performed on August 26 in Paris at église Saint-Louis en l'Île. The same date as the wedding. She had purchased two tickets online a month earlier, knowing very well that she could not attend, and certainly not with Libby. And so, why plan for this? Why print the tickets and stuff them in her suitcase? Because she knew all along that she would not attend the wedding? Not true. She had had every intention. But now, here she was, thinking about Mozart, pondering the unconscious motivations of a supposedly sentient woman.

She managed to find a room at a hotel in Montparnasse where a passport was not required. A small room that gave out onto rue Delambre where, early in the morning, the street cleaners appeared. On Friday, she went to the embassy and began the process for a temporary passport. On Saturday, she visited the Père-Lachaise cemetery and found the gravesite of Proust, where a young couple were taking turns reading from a book. She stood within hearing distance, but far enough away so as not to interfere, and she listened to the young woman read. She read in English, and her voice was clear and mellifluous, and she read with quiet passion. When she was done, she looked up and saw Lucille watching her. She smiled. The young man turned and beckoned for Lucille to come closer. She did. It turned out they were from Montréal, on their honeymoon, and they had sought out the cemetery because the woman had come here as a young girl, with her father, and she was trying to recall that time. She remembered the smell specifically. And the metro tickets scattered about in memoriam. And the various paths. The man took the young woman's hand and they walked off. The bare calves of the young woman were strong like a dancer's.

When she was younger, Lucille had started Proust. Morris had recommended it for its descriptions of longing and loss, but she had never finished it. She was halfway through the first volume. She took pleasure in remembering exactly where she had left off, and she knew that she could go back at any time and fall into the rhythm of the writing and get caught up once again in the lives of the characters. Though she felt no particular need to go back. It was simply enough to know that Proust would be permanently available. She thought of her own slim knowledge of Proust, and she thought of cemeteries in general. She still had Martin's ashes. In a small box in a drawer. She never looked at the box. But she knew where it was.

If she had wisdom, would she say that she knew her child was mortal? Twelve years after Martin's death, in the centre of Paris, she was finally thinking about grief and death again. Oh, she had felt grief often before, and she had tried thinking about it, but she would get distracted by her feelings, and so lose touch with her thinking. Grief was mental pain. It rested in the base of her skull. It fogged her brain. Grief and anger, pleasure and pain, delight and desire, fear and pity. The greatest of these was grief. But the mind was capable of healing itself. She believed this. If she didn't, what was the point in disputation, in mulling over, in regarding oneself, indeed in living?

She had first heard Mozart's Requiem performed when she was a student in Montréal. And then she'd heard it again when she and Libby had attended a performance in Winnipeg. Libby was seventeen at the time. And Libby had fallen in love with Mozart, and so then everything she listened to was Mozart, and by extension anything classical. She attempted to convert her friends to classical music, and a few went along for the ride, but most were into techno or some other type of music that Libby claimed was harsh and overwhelming and ultimately false.

Mozart composed the early movements of his Requiem in Vienna in 1791. It remained unfinished at his death in December of that year at the age of thirty-five, and was completed in 1792 by Franz Xaver Süssmayr, a student of Mozart's, who depended on the notes Mozart had passed on. After Mozart's death, his widow Constanze claimed that, at some point during the composition, Mozart said, I believe I am writing my own requiem.

On Sunday, the day of the concert, Lucille left her hotel early, planning to walk to the église Saint-Louis en l'Île. The concierge at the hotel had shown her on the map the best direction to take. Past le jardin du Luxembourg and right towards place du Panthéon and then left again towards pont de la Tournelle. He'd traced a line on the map so that she would not get lost. Forty minutes.

It was a warm day, and at some point, she shed herself of her sweater. She was wearing a sleeveless orange top, and dark navy pants with a slight flare that fell to just above her ankle, and she was wearing running shoes, and she carried in her newly purchased bag dress shoes into which she would change just after crossing the bridge. She wanted to be presentable for Mozart.

She wondered if she might sell one of her tickets, but then she thought better of it and she walked over to the wicket where a young woman was sitting, and she explained that she had an extra ticket. It had been intended for her daughter, but her daughter was not available, and so she would like for someone else to use it. She would leave it here, and if someone asked about a seat — of which there were none because the concert was sold out, she knew this — would the woman please give the ticket away for free. To whoever asked. Thank you. She said all of this quite slowly, and with much gesticulation and formality, and when she was done, she left the woman and entered the church. She asked for the toilets and was pointed in that direction. When she exited the bathroom, she heard the instruments warming up. She entered the auditorium of the church and found her seat. Her mouth was dry, perhaps from the lengthy walk, perhaps from nervousness. She took a small sip from her water bottle.

People were talking around her. She heard the voices but did not follow what anyone was saying. She was alone. The stage was empty. The audience was settling in. A young man made his way along the aisle towards her. He excused himself and pointed at the empty seat beside Lucille and asked in a stumbling French if it was free. Lucille nodded and said in English that it was. He sat. He looked about eagerly. His face was very young, very open, very attentive. He turned to Lucille and said in English that today was his lucky day. He had scored a free ticket. Those were his words. He told her that he had been in the south, but now he was visiting Paris, spending his time in the galleries, hanging out in the cemeteries. He said that August was the best time, for the people were all gone. He said that Mozart calmed the tumult of his mind. He smiled and said her name and asked her if she found that to be the case as well, that the tumult went away. Or perhaps tumult was only for the young. She wondered at that moment how he knew her name and realized that she must have told him right off, for he had asked her. And then said his own name. And now he was using her name, almost as a means of emphasis, or as if, by repeating her name, he might recollect her later. She did not remember his name. She couldn't ask again, it was too late, and so he was simply the young man.

He said that in June he had been living in southern France, at a hostel in La Grande Motte. One evening, he heard of a concert that was to take place in Montpellier. It was Erik Satie's *Socrate*, and because he loved Socrates and he loved Satie as well, it was as if the stars had aligned. On the day of the concert, he rented a bicycle and he wore his best jeans and shirt and his dress shoes. Exactly what he was wearing today. He set out in the afternoon. The concert was to begin at 7 p.m., and he didn't have a ticket, and he wanted to get there early to buy one. The young man paused, and smiled, and then said that it was a habit of his to show up at concerts without a ticket and hope that the gods would take care of him.

On that day, riding to Montpellier on his three-speed bicycle, which was cumbersome, he worried about not getting a ticket. And so, he pushed hard, and when he got to the theatre where the concert was to take place, he was sweaty and hot and dirty. When he entered the theatre, there were no people and the box office was closed. He looked around and finally found a security guard who was smoking outside, near the back entrance to the theatre. He approached the guard, who put out his cigarette, and stood to attention, and he asked the guard about the Satie concert. The guard shook his head and said that there was no Satie concert planned for the evening. It had in fact taken place the week previous.

The young man said that when he heard this news, he looked down at his feet and he saw that there was chain grease on his good pants. And then the guard said that, in any case, the concert had been completely sold out, and even if he had made it on time, and on the right day, his efforts would have been for nothing. The young man told Lucille that he left the theatre disappointed, but not sad. For he had the evening before him, and so he explored the city, and he ate mussels and fries in a small restaurant where he met an older couple who befriended him, and with whom he spent time drinking and eating and discussing the life of Stendhal. It is a strange thing, the young man said, to be disappointed, but then to have that disappointment replaced by conversation and wine and food and happiness and the discovery of new friends. Though *friends* is perhaps too optimistic, he said, for I never saw that couple again. They are gone. But I still see them in my head, and I recall their voices and their laughter, and I remember that they were both very generous thinkers, and they were in love, and I tell stories about them. And so, they are still with me.

At this point, the members of the orchestra and the choir entered. And then the four soloists. And finally, the conductor. The audience applauded. An acknowledgement that was neither too loud nor too quiet. The young man beside her slid forward in his seat. His jaw was quite defined. His hair needed washing. He wore dark dress shoes. And jeans. A light-blue button-down shirt. He was holding his breath, or so it seemed, for when the first sound was emitted from the orchestra, he exhaled, and he settled back in his chair. Crossed his legs like an old man. Lucille saw the grease on the cuff of his pants.

In the early movements, Lucille found that her thoughts were flying away. She willed herself back, and then she flew away again. She crossed her wrists in her lap in order to still her brain. And slowly, she relaxed. At some point, during the "Recordare," which contained the four soloists, she began to cry. The tears came unexpectedly, and she was discreet in her crying, but she was certainly crying, because her cheeks were wet, and her chest was heaving. No one seemed to notice, or maybe everyone was crying, she did not know. She did not care. The loneliness of the wind instruments, the beautiful dark-haired woman who sang alto, Mozart's intuition as he wrote his own requiem, the brilliance of artifice, which revealed beauty and truth. Loneliness again. Youth. Sadness and then happiness, and then more sadness and then more happiness. A strange peace.